NUMBER 88

Edited by

John P. Gunnison

© 2006 Adventure House

The Man Who Wasn't There Double Detective, August 1940. Copyright © 1940 by The Frank A. Munsey Company Copyright renewed © 1968 and assigned to Argosy Communications, Inc. "Double Detective" and its distinctive logo and symbolism and all related elements are trademarks and are the property of Argosy Communications, Inc. All Rights Reserved. Reprinted by arrangement with Argosy Communications, Inc.

Subscription Rate - $45.00 - 6 Issues - Advertising Rates - Full Page - $75.00. The publisher has made every effort to contact the present owners of any copyrighted material. Our apologies to those who hold such rights but whom we failed to contact because ownership was unknown or addresses were incomplete. Appropriate credit will be given in future editions if such copyright holders contact the publisher.

Printed in the United States of America

ISBN: 1-59798-036-6

First Adventure House Edition May 2006

HIGH ADVENTURE

We return once more to the world of The Green Lama. Also as a special added feature, we have three stories by that late horror master Hugh B. Cave to celebrate his last appearance at Windy City Pulp and Paperback Convention three years ago.

The Green Lama finds himself aboard a cruise ship sailing for Los Angeles and bound for the Panama Canal and the East Coast. What sets this tale apart from most of the other stories is that The Green Lama appears only as the Lama and his alternate identity of Dr. Charles Pali and not as Jethro Dumont. Written by Kendell Foster Crossen under the house name of Richard Foster, Crossen like Walter Gibson had a fascination with magic. According to the noted pulp historian, Wooda Carr, The Green Lama was supposed to be the Gray Lama. Being dressed in Gray, the Lama would be able to emulate The Shadow and sneak in and out of dark places. They changed him to Green because of cover art concerns. Sort of the cover deciding on plots prior to the stories even being written. Although a direct competitor to The Shadow, The Green Lama couldn't hold The Shadow's cloak and the magazine The Lama appeared in, DOUBLE DETECTIVE along with most all of the inventory being published by The Frank A. Munsey Company was sold to Popular Publications in 1943.

Hugh B. Cave was a world traveling pulp writer whose output was prodigious. Some of his best work appeared in the "Weird Menace" magazines, where he wrote for most of the titles, HORROR STORIES, TERROR TALES and THRILLING MYSTERY where all three of our stories in this issue comes from. The Thrilling group didn't have the niche down quite like Popular did and THRILLING MYSTERY was the only true "Weird Menace" title they produced. Cave's stories really don't alter much from the formula set forth by DIME MYSTERY, the father of all "Weird Menace" titles, and the number of weird doings and semi-plausible endings continue unabated with these three titles.

Happy Reading

John P. Gunnison
gunnison@adventurehouse.com

A Green Lama Story

The Man Who Wasn't There
By Richard Foster

Author's Note

THERE is something rather odd about the present monograph which I feel should be explained. I have been unable to find any trace of Jethro Dumont during the time the *S. S. Cathay* made its way from Los Angeles to New York. Dumont checked out of his hotel in Hollywood and

vanished. There is evidence of Tsarong returning on the train, but a check-up of trains, air lines and steamship lines fails to disclose a ticket sale to Jethro Dumont. Nevertheless, Jethro Dumont was back in New York shortly after the *S. S. Cathay* had docked at its pier in the North River.

Although there is no proof, I do have a couple of theories. The first one is that

The moonlight flashed on the weapon in the attacker's right hand

"Man Overboard!" The dreaded cry of the sea rang out through the night and thus began a series of circumstances, and the beginning of a gigantic plot that tested to the utmost the powers of The Green Lama

Dumont, for reasons of his own, wanted to return incognito and purchased a ticket under another name. This may have been to evade reporters who had trailed him since he was known to have stayed in Hollywood with his friend, Carter Mitchell,* when the latter was arrested.

The other theory, which fits in with my original assumption, is that Jethro Dumont is the Green Lama and therefore returned on the *S. S. Cathay* as Dr. Charles Pali. I am inclined to favor this theory in spite of the evidence to the contrary in *Babies For Sale*.* Otherwise I believe I would have discovered some record of Dumont's return.

This, however, as I have pointed out before, is purely a personal opinion and I have no evidence to back it up. I don't

* Readers will remember that Carter Mitchell was the director who was the real brains back of the gang whose operations were disclosed in the case of *Babies For Sale*.

* I am referring to the time when Jethro Dumont visited the sound stage, during the filming of a picture, and the Green Lama was seen to cross the back of the set.

want to influence the readers but believe it only fair to give all the facts and let them decide which is the more plausible.

R. F.

CHAPTER I

Man Overboard

SMOKE was already pouring from the funnels of the *S. S. Cathay* as she lay at her pier in Los Angeles. Within thirty minutes the small ship would draw in its gangplank, cast off and head southward for the Panama Canal. Passengers were hurrying aboard, and the decks were crowded with laughing, noisy visitors. There was such an air of activity that one could almost imagine the ship straining at her ropes, eager to be slipping out of the harbor and into the Pacific.

Three people came up the gangplank together. One of them, a man in his early forties, led the way to the purser's office. He was short, stockily-built, with black hair and a close-cropped black mustache. He wore light gray tweeds and a tweed cap, and puffed vigorously on a bulldog pipe. The young man and woman who followed him were obviously in love. The young man was tall and well-built, with a great shock of curly black hair, bared to the salty breeze. He was quite handsome in spite of a slightly crooked nose. The girl, a slender willowy blonde, clung to his arm and smiled up at him as he talked in an undertone.

"I am Dr. Harrison Valco," the older man said as they reached the purser. "This is Mr. Gary Brown and Miss Evangl Stewart. We have reservations for single cabins."

"Oh, yes," the purser answered, checking his list. "You are in Cabin 8, Dr. Valco. Miss Stewart is in Cabin 6 and Mr. Brown in Cabin 4. All on Deck A."

"Thank you," Dr. Valco said. The three of them followed a cabin steward up the stairs to the upper deck.

They had just left when a tall man, in the garb of a priest, stepped up. His face was ruddy and full, there was a slight touch of gray in his hair. His was the face of a man who was physically and spiritually content. Only the sharp upward curve of his eyebrows lent a touch of skepticism to an otherwise placid countenance. He was dressed in a dark green suit and wore an ecclesiastical shirt and collar in light green. On the front of the collar a strange symbol was embroidered in black. A student of the Orient would have recognized it as the Sanskrit symbol for *Om*.

"You have a reservation for Dr. Charles Pali?" * he asked softly.

The purser's pencil slid along the column of names and he nodded. His gaze rested momentarily on the ecclesiastical collar with its striking design, "Yes, Father Pali," he said. "Cabin 2, Deck A."

The green frocked priest followed a steward up the stairs while the purser turned to the next passenger.

The friends of passengers were slowly leaving the ship and a few minutes later the *S. S. Cathay* swung away from the pier and stuck her nose southward. Passengers lined the promenade deck and waved until Los Angeles dwindled to a toy village.

A young actor, who had been dissatisfied with his Hollywood success, took another look at the tall, red-headed girl next to him and made his way to the

---

* Rev. Pali was the name used by the Green Lama. Although I am convinced that the features of Dr. Pali were partly make-up, and the name evidently came from the *pali* dialect, the Green Lama was an ordained priest in the lamaist sect of Buddhism.

smoking room. A pretty young matron stopped waving at an already-invisible friend and went to her cabin. A San Francisco exporter looked at his watch and went into the bar for a quick Scotch and soda. Three well-dressed men left the rail together and asked a steward to bring a bottle down to the suite on Cabin B Deck which they shared together. Gary Brown and Evangl Stewart walked around the starboard side of the promenade deck and gazed out past the bow of the ship to where the ocean stretched to meet the sky. A tugboat tooted mournfully.

TO MOST people there is nothing quite so thrilling as the first dinner at sea. It represents the first opportunity to inspect the other travelers; to see who you are going to be cooped up with for the next two weeks; to talk about who is seated at the captain's able and speculate on why they were granted that privilege. To Gary and Evangl, sitting at a small table at one end of the dining room on Deck C, it was a double thrill since they were also seeing it for the first time through each other's eyes.

There was only one empty chair at the captain's table when the Green Lama, as Dr. Pali, entered the dining room and followed a steward to the big table. Captain Betts introduced himself and then each of the passengers at the table.

The rather plump, pretty blonde on the Lama's right was Mrs. Maryland Forbes; the slender girl, with the sultry beauty of the tropics, who sat on his left was Senorita Carmen Esteban; the sandy-haired man beyond her was Terrill Foran; on the other side of Mr. Foran was a young, red-headed woman who answered the introduction with a cynical smile; next was a Mr. Lerner,

a short heavy-set man, and his wife.

Mrs. Forbes on the captain's left had evidently been telling the captain all about her visit to Hollywood and about her husband who was in New York. She resumed her story, with exaggerated animation, chattering away at great length.

It wasn't until the meat course that she turned her attention to the man on her right. She lowered her voice for her first question.

"I hope you won't think I'm too inquisitive, Father Pali," she said, "but ever since you came in I've been wondering what church you represent. I can't remember ever having seen a priest with that strange-looking symbol on his collar."

The Green Lama smiled tolerantly. "I'm a Buddhist," he said.

"Oh, a Buddhist," she said vaguely. "That's in China or somewhere, isn't it?"

"There are many Buddhists there," the Lama admitted. "But I was trained in the lamaist sect in Tibet."

"But you look like an American," Mrs. Forbes exclaimed.

"I am," the Lama said, smiling.

"Pardon me," the sandy-haired Terrill Foran said, leaning forward, "did I hear you say you were a Buddhist?"

"That's right."

"A Buddhist priest?"

"Yes," the Green Lama answered.

"Then you can answer a question for me," Foran said. "I've been reading a little about the Buddhists lately but there are a couple of things I'd like to know. What's your stand on all the ceremonies they have over there to warn off heathen evils?"

"That can best be answered," the Green Lama said, "by telling you a story about the Buddha. That is, if you're interested?"

"Please do," the Senorita Esteban urged. The others at the table had stopped talking and were listening.

"Once," the Green Lama began, "on His way, the Blessed One, while staying at the bamboo grove near Rājāgriha, met Srigāla, a householder, who clasping his hands, turned to the four quarters of the world, to the zenith above and the nadir below. And the Blessed One knowing that this was done to avert evil, asked Srigāla, 'Why do you perform these strange ceremonies?'

"Srigāla answered, 'Do you think it strange that I protect my home against the demons? I know that thou, O Gotama Çākyamuni, whom people call the Tathāgata and the Blessed Buddha, wouldst tell me that incantations are of no avail. But know that in performing this rite I honor the sacred words of my father.'

"Then the Tathāgata said, 'You do well to keep sacred the words of your father. I find no fault with the performance of your father's rite. But I find that you do not understand the ceremony. Let the Tathāgata, who is now speaking to you as a spiritual father, explain to you the meaning of the six directions.

" 'To guard your home by mysterious ceremonies is not enough; you must guard it by good deeds. Turn to your parents in the east, to your Teachers in the south, to your wife and children in the west, to your friends in the north, and regulate the zenith of your religious relations above you and the nadir of your servants below you.

" 'Such is the religion your father desires you to have.'

"And Srigāla looked up to the Blessed One with reverence and said, 'Truly, Gotama, thou art Buddha, the Blessed One, the holy Teacher. I never

knew what I was doing but now I know. Thou hast revealed to me the truth that was hidden, as one who brings a lamp into the darkness. I take my refuge in the Enlightened Teacher, in the Truth that enlightens, and in the community of brethren who have found the truth.' " *

"I still don't know any more than I did before," the sandy-haired man grumbled.

"Maybe that's because you haven't found the truth yet," the red-headed girl said, grinning impishly. "Me, I think the Father's got something there."

"Tell me," the plump Mrs. Forbes said, "is it true that you can do all sorts of things, like astral projection for instance?"

"There are many things which are true, yet you would not believe them," the Green Lama answered gravely.

"Say," Foran said again, "if you're a Buddhist, maybe you know something about this Green Lama that the Los Angeles papers have been mentioning."

"Oh yes, I read about him," Mrs. Forbes exclaimed. "Isn't he a criminal?"

"I know little about him," the Lama said, "but I doubt if he has criminal intentions."

"You have spent some time in Tibet?" Senorita Esteban asked, as though to lead the conversation away from religion. The Green Lama answered her and for several minutes there was general talk on Tibet. Then the conversation shifted to other topics.

IT WAS still early in the evening, although dinner had been over some time when the Green Lama left his

* This story told by the Green Lama may be found in Seven Falls Sutras, pages 297 to 320.

cabin. He stopped and tapped on Gary's door. Gary threw the door open.

"Hello, chief," he said. "I thought maybe you were Evangl. We're going out for a few turns around the deck."

He walked over to the dresser and finished knotting his tie. Then he reached into a drawer and started to draw out a holster with a heavy automatic in it. With an embarrassed laugh, he dropped it back."

"I've been wearing that so long," he said, "that I don't feel dressed without it. But this is almost like a vacation. Guess I won't need it."

The Green Lama smiled from across the stateroom. "It is just as well," he said, "to divorce yourself from weapons of violence, but I am not so sure that this will be like a vacation."

"What's up?" Gary asked. His hand went back into the drawer and brought out the holster and gun. He began buckling it under his armpit. "Did you hear something?"

"No, but there is a feeling of evil on this boat. It is written that the wise man senses evil even before it arrives."

"I don't feel anything," Gary said.

"A man in love is not a wise man," the Green Lama said dryly. "Perhaps the evil will not manifest itself on the boat, but it is here."

"Maybe you're right at that," Gary said. "I didn't think anything of it at the time but I saw a guy down in the dining room I used to know. Carlos Lopez. He used to sell reefers to the Harlem dealers. There was some kind of a blow-off over his men selling the reefers to school kids and he left town. Later, I heard he'd quit the racket and went straight."

"That is doubtful," the Green Lama said. "If the cloth be dirty, however much the dyer might dip it into blue, yellow, red or lilac dye its color will be

ugly and unclean—why? Because of the dirt in the cloth." *

"Yeah, you're probably right," Gary said. "He's a smooth customer too."

"What is written will be," the Lama said, rising. "In the meantime, I'll go

Mrs. Maryland Forbes

walking on the deck and let you take up the thread of your romance."

"Say, chief," Gary said as the Green Lama was going out the door, "you got any idea how much a small farm close to New York might cost?"

"A small farm?" the Green Lama asked. There was a twinkle in his eyes as he looked back. "Why a small farm?"

"Well," Gary said, "Evangl and I have decided to get married when we get back to New York whether her mother likes the idea or not. I thought maybe we could get a small farm close by and live there. Then I could still help you . . ."

"We'll see," the Lama promised. He turned and went out on deck.

*The Green Lama was quoting direct from volume 1, page 36 of Majjhima Nikaya.

It was quiet outside, with only the distant throb of motors faintly reaching the ears. Under his feet, the Green Lama could feel the slight vibration of the boat cutting through the water. Two or three other people were on deck, standing at the rail looking up at the star-studded sky. The Green Lama leaned his elbows on the rail and smiled as the wind struck his face. Off in the distance he could see the lights of a coastwise steamer going north.

He sensed someone beside him and glanced around. It was the Senorita Carmen Esteban. The faint fragrance of an elusive perfume reached him as he turned his head.

"Good evening, Father Pali," she said. There was no trace of Spanish accent.

"Good evening, O Magga," the Green Lama said.

She laughed lightly, throwing her head back to let the wind cool her face. "You are becoming more observant, *Tulku*," * she said. "Before, I always had to tell you who I was. Now you know the second time you see me. Am I getting more careless in my appearance?"

"Not at all," the Lama said. "But you looked far too understanding when I was telling the story of Gotama Cakyamuni at the dinner table. That, coupled with your perfume, told me that you could be only the Revealer of Secret Paths, the Magga."

"Well done, *Tulku*," she said. Then her manner became more serious. "Tell me, *Tulku*, do you also feel the presence of evil on this ship?"

The Green Lama did not seem surprised. "Yes," he said. "I have felt it since I came aboard. But it was stronger in the dining room."

"I too," Magga said. "It was as

* A lama of high rank.

though some person at the table . . ."

It was then that the quiet of the ship was shattered with a shout coming from the starboard side of the promenade deck. It was a shout—tinged with hysteria—that all seamen dread to hear:

"Man overboard! Man overboard!"

CHAPTER II

The Death's Head Ring

THE cry was taken up in other parts of the ship and within a few seconds there was a mighty jerk as the ship's engines were reversed and the liner was brought to a stop. A huge searchlight flashed on and began sweeping the waters. As a boat was lowered, passengers came running out of the lounge and crowded along the rail.

The whole effect was ghostly: the lighted ship surrounded by a thick, unending wall of darkness—and then that slender finger of light pushing through slowly, like a giant hand, feeling blindly for something lost. The passengers could see the boat, like a tiny peanut shell, tossing around on the waves below. It seemed as though hours went by, although in reality it was about thirty minutes, until the small boat finally pulled alongside the ship and was hoisted aboard. It contained only the sailors who had left in it. The passengers began talking excitedly as the men went in to report.

". . . a feeling of evil," Magga muttered under her breath.

The Green Lama nodded. "It has already struck," he said.

They were still standing at the rail talking when a steward approached a few minutes later.

"The captain would like to see all the passengers in the lounge," he said.

"The check-up to see who's missing," the Green Lama said. He and Magga walked to the front of the ship and entered the lounge. They felt the ship quiver as it once more got under way.

Most of the passengers were already inside, standing around in little groups. The purser was going around with his list, checking. The Green Lama glimpsed Evangl and Gary across the room with Dr. Valco. The red-headed Jean Farrell and Mrs. Forbes were standing next to the Lama.

"Isn't this too terrible, Father," Mrs. Forbes said, turning to him. "Just going off and leaving that poor man floundering back there in the sea somewhere."

"He was probably drowned before the boat was lowered," the Green Lama said gravely.

"It's terrible," Mrs. Forbes repeated. "I wasn't very far away and I even heard the poor man cry out as he fell. When my husband hears about this he's sure to forbid my taking another boat trip."

"Who was it gave the alarm?" Magga asked.

"Why, I believe it was Mr. Foran, who is at our table," Mrs. Forbes said. "He was standing not far from me and he must have seen the poor man fall."

"Yeah," Jean Farrell said, speaking for the first time, "if you ask me, he might have even helped with just a little push."

"Goodness!" Mrs. Forbes exclaimed. "That's a dreadful thing to say about a man who seems as nice as Mr. Foran."

"Well," Jean Farrell said calmly, "any guy who makes a pass at a girl before he's even through the shrimp course is in the money for pushing people overboard too. What do you say, Senorita Esteban?"

"Well," Magga said, "it is a little premature for what you call a pass."

"You bet. A respectable girl doesn't expect it until at least the dessert course. Oh-oh, here comes my shadow."

"Quite a mess, eh?" the young man said as he came up to them. He was a tall, slender, good-looking young man, with close-cropped brown hair.

"This is Ken Clayton, God's gift to autograph hounds," Jean Farrell said as she introduced them. "He's the only man I know who not only will not admit he looks like Robert Taylor but who also refuses to be built into a Hollywood glamor boy. He looks like Robert Taylor but he wants to be a Paul Muni."

"Oh, you're an actor," Mrs. Forbes said breathlessly.

"That's what I thought," Ken Clayton said, "but Hollywood thought differently. So it's back to Broadway for me."

"Look," Magga said. "They must have discovered who's missing. They're letting everyone go."

Most of the passengers were filing out of the lounge, their faces mirroring disappointment at not being told all the morbid details.

The Green Lama wandered over to where Captain Betts was standing.

"Did you learn who the unfortunate person was, Captain?" he asked.

"None—" began the captain, whirling around. "Oh, I'm sorry, Father. I thought you were one of the gossips." He lowered his voice. "Yes, he was a Mr. Robert Walters from New York, a lawyer, although I can't learn much more about him. The purser remembers his coming aboard at San Francisco but not much about his appearance. A nondescript man, I guess. He failed to come down to dinner and so no one saw him from the time he came aboard until the accident."

"Who gave the alarm?" the Green Lama asked.

"Mr. Foran who was at dinner with us," the captain said. "He was standing on the starboard deck and just caught a glimpse of the body going overboard."

"Have you looked through his things?" the Lama wanted to know.

"One of the stewards just did. He found only the usual things a man takes on a trip. Nothing to indicate a suicidal intention—or motive."

"What do you do with his things?"

"They'll be locked in his cabin," the captain said, "and turned over to his relatives. His papers show that they live in New York. We'll radio them tonight."

"A terrible tragedy," the Green Lama said. "By the way, what cabin was he in?"

"Cabin 14 on Deck B. Why do you ask, Father?" There was an odd expression on the captain's face and the Green Lama noticed his quick exchange of glances with the purser who was standing beside him.

"Just curiosity," the Green Lama said. "There is an old saying in Tibet that a man who dies suddenly or violently hates to give up his earthly abode and will return to it for three nights."

"Well, he won't be able to get in with the door locked," the purser said, laughing. But the Green Lama was aware of a nervousness under the laughter. Certainly, he thought, an ordinary superstition wouldn't produce that. But he thanked the captain and went through the lounge to his cabin.

IN THE Green Lama's cabin there was a small Buddha shrine, no more than a foot high, in one corner. In front of it a small butter-candle, flickering in the wind that came through the open porthole, filling the room with its salty tang. The Green Lama seated himself, crosslegged, on the floor in front of it. For the next hour the only sound in the room was the low-voiced chant of the Green Lama and the clicking of the prayer wheel around his neck.

It was quite late when the Green Lama rose from the floor and went to the stateroom wardrobe. From it he took a long green robe, put it on and adjusted the hood. It was dark green silk, lined on the inside with golden yellow, and there was a band of green fur around the sleeves and the hood. Next a dark red *kata*, or scarf, went around his neck. The Green Lama was ready for action.

He opened the door and slipped silently into the corridor. He closed the door behind him and stood there for a moment, listening carefully. The passageway was empty. Then, seeming to blend with the very shadows, he slipped through the lounge, into the foyer and down the stairs that led to Deck B. The stairway led him down into the foyer on the lower deck directly before the darkened purser's office. Cabin 14 was on his left, directly in front of one of the suites.

Then he heard footsteps along the foyer. The Green Lama, moving with incredible speed, darted noiselessly to the shadow of the purser's doorway and stood there, hugging the wall, while a man, wearing an officer's uniform, came by and passed out of sight up the stairway.

The Green Lama waited a moment until he was sure there was no one else coming and then he went along the foyer until he came to Cabin 14. In a moment he was bending down to the keyhole, a small sliver of steel in his hand. There was a slight rasp as the tiny pick began fumbling for the tumblers of the lock.

As he felt the door begin to give, the Lama heard, or rather sensed, someone behind him. He straightened and whirled—but too late. He caught a brief glimpse of a hand and then something crashed on the top of his skull. He crumpled to the floor. Through his fading consciousness footsteps scuffed hurriedly away, away.

He had no idea how long he had been lying there on the floor of the foyer. There was a huge lump on the side of his head and his head was aching. It had been a terrific blow and the fact that he was turning as the blow fell had probably saved his life. He felt on the floor for his steel pick and tried the door to Cabin 14. It swung open at his touch.

Despite the pain in his head, and the dizziness from the blow, he entered the cabin and carefully went through everything in it. There were two suitcases filled with clothes; a briefcase containing a bundle of legal papers, and a smaller case with an insurance policy on Robert Walters, made out to Laura Walters, a driver's license, and a few odds and ends of personal identification papers. On the dressing table was a picture of a rather pleasant-faced woman and a small child. A copy of the Los Angeles *Times* of the day before was folded on a chair, but there seemed to be nothing particularly significant in that.

At last, satisfied that the room held no secret, the Green Lama stepped into the foyer and locked the door. Then he slipped up the stairway and down the hall to Dr. Valco's stateroom, three doors beyond his.

Dr. Valco, wearing a dressing gown, answered his light tap.

"I say, what's up?" he asked as the Green Lama came into the room.

"I can't tell yet," the Green Lama answered, "but someone gave me a scalp massage with a blackjack." He sank into a chair.

"Here, let me see," Valco said. He pulled the hood back and began feeling the lump on the Lama's head.

Dr.
Harrison
Valco

"I want you to do something," the Green Lama said as Dr. Valco examined him. "I've already asked too many questions; if I ask more they may become suspicious. Tomorrow, see if you can learn what stateroom Carlos Lopez is in. Gary says that Lopez used to be with a gang in New York. It's expecting too much of coincidence to think that he's aboard without having something to do with whatever is going on."

"Aren't you jumping at conclusions?" Valco asked. "There's nothing to show the man didn't commit suicide."

"Then why was I attacked?" the Green Lama asked.

"That is strange," Valco admitted.

"Maybe you're right." Valco nodded.

"Another thing, Doctor; see if you can learn the mystery of Cabin 14. There's something definitely wrong there, by the action of the captain and the purser. You might get chummy with the ship's doctor and get the story out of him."

"That's an idea," Valco said. He finished dabbing some iodine on the Lama's head. "That'll be all right by morning. There's just a slight break in the skin. But if the blow had been more direct, it might have been serious. Have you any idea who took a swing at you?"

"No," the Green Lama admitted. "I sensed someone behind me and started to turn as he struck. All I saw was a brief glimpse of a hand. It could have been a man or a woman. There was only one mark of identification and he'll be too smart to let me see that again."

"What was it?"

"A ring. A death's head ring, but a very peculiar one; suggested the badge of some society. It was a small jade skull placed within an inverted pentagram* of raised silver."

"A death's head!" exclaimed Valco. "What do you think that means? A cult of some sort?"

"I doubt it. Probably no more than a means of identification for some gang. You won't forget to dig up that information tomorrow?" The Green Lama rose and went to the door.

"Right," Valco said.

"Om! Vajra Sattva!"** the Green Lama said.

"Good night," Dr. Valco said, but the Green Lama had already vanished into the dark hallway.

*The inverted pentagram was once used as a symbol by the worshippers of Black Magic. See An Analysis of Magic and Witchcraft by C. W. Olliver, page 46.
**A variation of Om! Ma-ni pad-me Hum!

CHAPTER III

In Suite A

IT WAS after lunch the following day before the Rev. Dr. Pali was seen by the other passengers. By that time the lump had disappeared from the side of his head and all the after-effects of the attack were gone. He walked down to Deck B and watched the swimmers in the pool for several minutes. Gary and Evangl were there, as was the red-headed Jean Farrell. At length the green-clad priest turned back into the foyer and up the stairs.

He made his way to the front of the promenade deck and leaned against the rail, staring out at the sea. Far below him the green-blue water tossed restlessly as the ship slid through it. A half mile off to his right a fruit boat slowly plowed through the ocean toward Los Angeles. The S. S. Cathay was still fairly close to land and occasionally a sea gull would swoop around the ship, following in the hope that some scraps would be thrown out.

Behind him the Green Lama heard the soft scuff of feet and caught the faint fragrance of a subtle perfume.

"Greetings, O Magga," he said softly, without turning.

"Tashi shog,* Tulku," Magga answered as she leaned against the rail beside him.

"I heard about last night," she said after several minutes of silence. "Tulku, you should be more careful. What if you had been killed?"

"After I am gone others will spring up in the path of evil," he said. "Have you learned anything?"

"A little," Magga said. "Also I just

*"May prosperity be"—a Tibetan greeting.

saw Dr. Valco. I made myself known to him. He said to tell you that Carlos Lopez is in Suite A on Deck B. He is sharing it with Terrill Foran, the sandy-haired man who sat at our table last night, and a James Nord. These three are supposed to be Los Angeles business men on their way to the World's Fair."

"Did he learn anything about Cabin 14?" the Green Lama asked.

"Yes. He found out why the captain acted so oddly when you were asking him about it. This is the third man who's gone overboard from that cabin."

"The third!" exclaimed the Green Lama. "No wonder the purser looked so nervous when I mentioned superstition. Who were the others?"

"Just ordinary business men like this one."

"Each of them vanished on eastward trips?"

"No," Magga said. "The first one went overboard two days out of New York on the westward trip. That was about three months ago. The second man disappeared on an eastward trip about the same place as this one did."

"Maybe it's to get their insurance," the Green Lama said, remembering the policy that he had seen in the cabin the night before.

"Dr. Valco thought of that," Magga said, "and asked the ship's doctor about it. He said that neither of the first two men carried insurance. That the liner officials had also thought of that and had investigated. The sailors are beginning to say that particular cabin is bad luck."

"It was for at least three men," the Green Lama said dryly.

"I've got more news though," Magga said. "This morning there was a very quiet search of the ship. Apparently it yielded nothing and the officers gave no reason. But the purser has an eye for Spanish beauty and I managed to find out what it was all about. The captain received a radio from the Los Angeles police this morning. The head of a national smuggling ring is on board the *Cathay*. The L. A. police have been after this ring for several months and thought they finally had it sewed up. When they closed in last night their bird had flown, but they found a clue that pointed here. The only hitch is that they don't know who the head of the ring is. So Captain Betts was playing hide-and-seek all morning."

"And?" prompted the Green Lama, guessing from her attitude that she had more to tell.

"AND, on my own," Magga said, "I found out that part of the smuggling ring is on board; namely, the three gentlemen in Suite A. On top of that, the first mate, whose name is Shallet, is in the ring too. There's going to be a meeting some time tonight in the suite. I couldn't find out the exact time though."

"I'll be there," the Green Lama said. "Maybe one of the three men is the leader."

"Don't forget," Magga warned, "that it might also be a woman. That red-headed girl was talking to me this morning and kept steering the conversation around to you. I felt that she was trying to pump me although there's no reason why she should think there's any connection between us."

"I have a feeling," the Green Lama said, "that the answer to everything will lie in the man who went overboard last night."

"Maybe he was one of the gang and they just wanted to get rid of him."

"And the other two?"

"I cannot guess," Magga said.

"No," the Lama said again, shaking his head, "the answer is in the mystery of the man from Cabin 14. If I could only find it. . . . O Wisdom that is gone, gone, gone to the beyond, and beyond the beyond: Svâhâ!.. .*"

"There is also a rumor making the rounds," Magga said, "that the Green Lama was seen on the boat last night."

"Probably started by whoever it was that attacked me last night," the Lama said. "You have seen the men who are Foran's conspirators?"

"Yes. Shallet, the first mate, is a huge, shaggy man with close-cropped blond hair. Lopez is a little, snaky-looking man with black hair and a waxed mustache. Nord is a tall, skinny man with a face like a death's head."

"Like a death's head," repeated the Green Lama. "Do any of them wear a death's head ring?"

"They don't need one as long as they have Nord around," Magga said. "Why do you ask?"

"The one who struck me wore such a ring. Since we know Foran is in the gang, do you suppose suspicion prompted his remarks about the Green Lama last night?"

"That might be it," Magga said. "He's quite a lad. The Farrell girl was right about him. He's already made three passes at me and a couple at Evangl. Gary is ready to take a swing at him."

"Warn Gary to check his temper. And now you had better go before someone thinks that Father Pali has forsaken his prayer wheel for the castanets of Senorita Esteban."

"You are going to the suite to-night?" Magga asked.

"Yes."

"Be careful, Tulku," she said softly.

"Remember the words of the Cikshasa-muccaya, 'Vigilance is the road to immortality. Negligence is the road to death.' "

"I will remember," the Green Lama said. "Om! Ma-ni pad-me Hum hri!"* He clicked the prayer wheel that hung around his neck.

"Om!" Magga said, and was gone.

THE sun was setting lower and lower in the west, its red-tinged rays sparkling on the water, when the Green Lama left the promenade deck and entered the foyer. He went on through the lounge and into his own stateroom. There, in front of the Buddha shrine, he squatted on the floor. For several minutes there was no sound other than the rhythmic clicking of the prayer wheel. Then his voice rose softly in a chant.

"Salutation to the Buddha.
"In the language of the gods and in that of the lus,
"In the language of the demons and that of the men,
"In all the languages which exist,
"I proclaim the Doctrine. . ."

His voice went on and on in the steady monotone of a chant as the butter-candle flamed brightly and the contented face of the Buddha looked down upon him.

On, through the dinner hour and long afterward, the low-voiced chanting continued. As the stateroom grew dark, the dancing flame of the butter-candle threw strange shadows over the walls and once it seemed almost as though the Buddha smiled and nodded at his disciple. Then again the room was silent except for the clicking prayer wheel.

At length the Green Lama rose from

---

* The Green Lama was quoting from the mantra of praise to the Prajnaparamita.

* Adding the hri to the prayer is for emphasis; it is equivalent to saying the prayer several times.

the floor and went to the wardrobe and put on the long, green monk's robe. He pulled the hood over his head and stepped out into the foyer.

There were several people still sitting in the lounge, so the Green Lama turned to the right and entered the empty lobby at the other end where another staircase led down to the next deck. Through the doorway he could glimpse several passengers in the barroom and in the smoking room beyond. But none of them saw the shadowy figure that slipped noiselessly through the lobby and down the stairs. Nor did any of them hear the slight whisper that seemed to echo in the lobby for several seconds after his passing: *"Om! Vajra guru pad-me siddhi Hum!"* *

Once on Deck B, the Green Lama sped silently past the barber shop and down the long corridor to the bow-end of the deck. He found Suite A on the starboard side. He stopped by the first door and listened intently. He was able to distinguish the slight murmur of voices. He moved on to the next door, leading into the second room of the suite. Again he listened at the door. Nothing was audible there.

From a pocket in the robe he took the tiny sliver of steel and bent over the lock. In a minute the door swung inward and the Green Lama stepped into the dark room. Across the room the door was open and he could clearly hear the men in the next room.

". . . and you'll be smart," a voice, that he recognized as Foran's, was saying, "if you just forget that you ever had any curiosity about the boss. It's healthier to keep your mind on business. Otherwise you may be following the path of our Mr. Walters and it'll be a damn sight less profitable."

_____
* Another, and longer, version of *Om! Ma-ni pad-me Hum!*, or *Hail! The Jewel in the Lotus Flower!*

Standing motionless in the dark room, the Green Lama listened to the conversation of the four men. He'd been there several minutes when he heard a chair scrape and one of the men said, "It's in the next room. I'll get it."

Jean Farrell

The Green Lama darted across the room to the door and slipped into the hallway. As he closed the door an eerie whisper seemed to fill the room, *"Om! Ma-ni pad-me Hum!"*

SOME time after dinner, three men were seated around a table in the sitting room of Suite A of the *S. S. Cathay*. One of them was Terrill Foran, the big sandy-haired man who had been at the captain's table in the dining salon. Next to him was a small, swarthy man with a waxed mustache. Across from them sat a tall man whose face looked like a death's head.

"Where the hell's Shallet?" the little man asked, scowling at his watch. "He should have been here twenty minutes ago."

"Take it easy, Lopez." the sandy-haired man said. "The way you act someone would think that you smoke your own reefers."

"He does," the other man said laconically. "One of these days the boss is going to get worried about that and have our little friend's head snicked off."

"Aw, shut up!" snapped Lopez. "None of your business what I do. There's plenty of reason to be nervous, what with the captain snooping around looking for the boss and us sittin' here with our pockets full. Maybe he's already got Shallet. If that ain't enough gotta have that damned Green Lama around too!"

"I'll admit," Foran said smoothly, "that something ought to be done about the Green Lama. He must be that fellow who calls himself Father Pali. It's too much to believe that there are two Buddhists on this boat at once—and one of them invisible. Something will have to be done all right, but it's up to the boss to say when."

There was a light knock on the door. Foran got up and admitted a huge, blond man dressed in the uniform of a first mate.

"Sorry I'm so late," the newcomer said, "but the old man had me cornered and insisted on talking my damned ear off about this hidden smuggler."

"Lopez was just about to jump through the porthole," Foran said. "He's got the reefer jitters."

"To tell the truth," the first mate said, "I got the jitters myself and they don't come from any weed. The old man is determined that he ain't going to have any smugglers on his ship. He's

gonna raise hell and high water looking."

"No need to worry," Foran said. "The boss won't be found."

"Just for once," the mate said, "I'd like to know who the boss is. I ain't too hot on this business of working for somebody that's invisible anyway, but when I have to help search for him, I want to know who he is."

"None of us know either," Foran said. "I've been in the gang for five years without knowing. But I've seen several guys that got curious—only I ain't seen them since, and you'll be smart if you just forget that you ever had any curiosity about the boss. It's healthier to keep your mind on business."

"Okay," the mate said sullenly, "only I still don't like it, see. I ain't curious but I ain't likin' it either."

"Just keep it to yourself, Shallet, and you'll be all right. In the meantime, the boss figures we got nothing to worry about so far as our pickups are concerned in Cristobal and Havana. The biggest worry is about what we've already got. It's too early to put it away yet and the captain's liable to get suspicious of us and search the stateroom. I might be able to head it off, but then again I might not."

"Yeah," Shallet grunted. "You can get by all right but Lopez looks like a snowbird."

"You big punk—" began Lopez.

"Shut up," Foran interrupted quietly, but with enough force to make Lopez sink back in his chair.

"You see, things like that," the mate said.

"Yeah, I know," Foran said. "So does the boss. So here's the idea. You'll take the box and keep it in your quarters until after we pass Havana. They'll never think of searching you."

"I don't like it," Shallet began.

"The boss doesn't ask you to like it," Foran said. "But you'll do it." There was an implacable harshness to his voice as he said this last.

"Okay," Shallet said. "Give it to me."

"It's in the next room," Nord said. "I'll get it." He pushed back his chair and started for the other room. Halfway there, he halted abruptly, his hand going to his pocket. "What was that?" he said.

"What?" demanded Foran.

"I HEARD somebody whisper in that room," Nord said. His hand came out gripping an automatic. "Something that sounded like 'omany.'"

Foran cursed under his breath. "Om ma-ni! That's part of a prayer that damn Green Lama's supposed to be always muttering. Get in there and look for him!"

As Nord obeyed, Foran leaped to the door leading into the foyer, a gun in his hand. He jerked open the door and looked out. When he saw nothing, he stepped outside and looked all around.

"Nothing out here," he said, going back into the stateroom.

"Same in here," Nord called from the next room, which was now lighted. "But wasn't this door locked?"

"I think so," Foran said.

"Well, it's unlocked now so maybe he was in here. I wonder how much he heard?"

"I'm tellin' you I don't like this," little Lopez said, his voice shrill with nervousness. "I've read about this guy. He ain't playin' for marbles! Every gang he's come up against has ended up on a marble slab, or in the can. Let's throw the stuff overboard and forget the whole thing!"

The man with a face like a death's head came back into the room and stood looking down at Lopez. There was a strange grin on his face. With one hand he was holding a steel box about a foot square, but his gun was still hanging lightly from the other hand.

"I don't know," he said, speaking to Foran without taking his eyes from Lopez, "but I've been thinkin' maybe Lopez is workin' too hard. Maybe we ought to send him on a little vacation."

Lopez shrank back in his chair under the steady, unemotional stare of Nord. "No," he said shrilly. "I'm okay —I was only kiddin'. Foran, you know I was only kiddin'. Tell him—"

"Lay off, Nord," Foran said. "We can't do anything without the boss sayin' okay anyway."

"The hell we can't," Nord said. His gaze shifted to the big first mate. "How about you, chum?" he asked. "You think we ought to be good boys too?"

Shallet wet his lips nervously and tried to smile. His face was pale. "No," he said. "I ain't got no kick coming."

"That's the spirit," Foran said. He nodded at Nord and the latter put his gun away and sat down at the table again. Little Lopez ran one hand through his hair, and inched his chair away as Nord looked at him again. Lopez was a killer himself, but he had to get hopped up on marijuana first, while he knew from experience that Nord was a completely unemotional executioner who needed nothing before or after to steady his nerves. It was too much for the little Mexican in his present state, with even the very air seeming to pluck at his nerves. He fidgeted, wishing he could get away for a quick smoke.

"Here's the stuff," Nord said, shoving the steel box across the table toward Shallet. The first mate took it reluctantly.

"You can hide it in your quarters," Foran said, "until the captain has given up his snooping, or until we get past Havana. Then we'll make the plant."

"Okay," Shallet said. "I better be getting back now. The old man might get suspicious if he happens to start looking for me."

"Sure," Foran said, waving his hand. "Beat it. But take good care of that box. It's worth damn near as much as this ship."

"And watch them cold feet of yours," Nord added. "I've known a lot of guys that got cold feet and it was fatal."

The big mate got up and left without answering. As soon as the door had closed behind him, Foran turned back to the others.

"You two guys scram," he said. "The boss is coming down here to see me. There's several things to be decided, including what to do with that Green Lama. I'll come up to the smoking room as soon as the boss is through."

Lopez and Nord got up and left the room. Lopez began fumbling in his pocket for a marijuana cigarette as he went through the door.

CHAPTER IV

For Davey Jones' Locker

 OUR days passed, uneventful but electric with suspense. The Green Lama spent his nights roaming the decks of the *S. S. Cathay*, listening in on the conversations in Suite A on Deck B, but without learning anything of importance. The men talked of when they would reach Cristobal and mention was made of someone named Miguel in Havana, but the references were so vague the Lama could draw little

from them. He spent his days in Cabin 2, having all of his meals served there. The impression in the dining room was that Father Pali was suffering from a slight attack of seasickness. During the day he slept and recited *mantras** and the *Ti Sarana** *. Dr. Valco and Magga brought him what meager information they could gather and even Gary and Evangl occasionally managed to stop gazing into each other's eyes long enough to drop by with something they thought might fit into the puzzle. But it all added up to nothing.

The Green Lama felt sure that evil plans were brooding. He sensed it, a feeling as though the criminals on the deck below were merely holding their peace until the right time. Several times when he left his cabin at night, he felt that he was watched but even his keen eyes failed to discover anyone.

He was certain that the conversation he had heard that one night in the suite below had referred to the smuggling of dope; that the box the men had given the first mate had contained narcotics. He could have easily slipped into the mate's quarters and gotten the box but he thought it more important to wait and find out what the whole scheme was. And to learn the identity of the mysterious boss who was unknown even to the members of the gang. He was also sure that there was more to the gang than just the smuggling of dope. And there was still the unanswered mystery of the Mr. Walters who had gone overboard that first night; whose wife and child would be waiting in New York for the return of his belongings.

It was fairly early in the evening of

* Buddist prayers.
** The Threefold Refuge, a part of the *Von Mahinda* for meditation. This is the one that begins: "*Buddham saranam gacchami, Dhammam saranam gacchami, Sangham saranam gacchami. . .*"

the seventh day out of Los Angeles when there was a slight tapping on the door of Cabin 2. The Green Lama already attired in his green robe, with the hood thrown back on his shoulders, was seated in front of the Buddha shrine. He rose and went to the door. It was the Senorita Carmen Esteban —Magga.

"Greetings, O Magga," he said as she entered and closed the door.

"Greetings, *Rimpoche**," she answered gravely. "There will be no need for you to go below tonight."

"Why?" he asked.

"The meeting was early," Magga said. "I just came from there. Tonight even the leader was present."

"He is—?"

"I don't know. I could see within the room but he was heavily muffled around the face and sat in the darkness. But I saw the death's head ring you mentioned. It must have been the boss who struck you down the night you entered the cabin of the missing man."

"None of the others wore such a ring?"

"No."

"What did you learn?" the Green Lama asked.

"SEVERAL things. There is need of you tonight, *Tulku*—need to prevent murder. The first mate, Shallet, was there and reported that his next in command, a second mate named Martin, is suspicious of him. He thinks that Martin caught a glimpse of the box he hid and he's afraid that Martin will go to the captain. The boss pronounced a death sentence—to be carried out on the bridge tonight around two in the

morning. I have seen many things, *Tulku*, but even I shuddered a little at the cold-blooded way that unknown man was sentenced to execution."

"It has been written that those who trade with Death have no fear of receiving short measure," the Green Lama said. "Were you able to recognize the voice of the Hidden One?"

"No," Magga said. "All orders were issued in a whisper that might have been the voice of anyone. But the fact that I heard that whisper and saw the hands disproves our first theory that the unknown boss might not exist— might be Foran himself."

"Not necessarily," the Green Lama said. "The voice could have been just that, to impress the hirelings. But it probably isn't Foran. Who was appointed the executioner of the second mate?"

"Lopez, the Mexican. He was already fortified with marijuana. He is to slip up behind Martin at two, when he will be on the bridge, and knife him. But Shallet and Foran are to go along to see that he does a good job and to help throw the body overboard."

"Did they plan how to cover up this murder?" the Green Lama asked.

"Yes, *Tulku*. This Lopez appears to be a man of many accomplishments and has already forged a suicide note which will be found in the quarters of the second mate. In it he will tell how he became mixed up with the smuggling ring but now is ashamed of having disgraced his family and his uniform and is taking the only way out. The note will be in his handwriting and addressed to the captain."

"Very clever," the Green Lama admitted.

"But that is not all," Magga said. "They decided that something had to be done about you and so in the suicide

* Precious one. While this term of address is usually thought of as applying only to the Dalai Lama in Tibet— the present, or 14th reincarnation of Buddha, is a six-year-old boy who was enthroned October 1939 at the Norbhu Lingka Palace in Lhasa——it is also occasionally used to address any lama of high rank.

note the second mate will name the hidden boss of the ring, the man the Los Angeles police radioed about, and the name in the note will be that of the Green Lama—Rev. Charles Pali."

"I suspected something of the sort," the Green Lama said. "The head of this smuggling ring is too clever to attack me directly unless it is necessary. Kill a priest and you infuriate the people; unfrock a priest and you win followers. Coupled with the bad newspaper publicity* the Green Lama received in Los Angeles, it might be difficult for me to prove that I'm not the smuggler. Either way, they force me into prison for a time or make me a fugitive on the ship, which they think will serve them as well."

"Before," Magga said, "there was always at least one member of the gang who knew who the man at the top was, but here there seems to be no one who knows him. It makes it even more difficult."

"With patience the hunter always drives the fox into the open," the Green Lama said. "So with patience, we shall eventually discover the identity of the Hidden One. It is written that a person cannot walk in complete darkness without treading on sharp stones."

"True," Magga admitted. "For a moment I forgot. Once you have stopped the murder of the man Martin, you must remember to get the note from his cabin. Or I can get it while you are on deck."

"No," the Lama said. "It is better that you do not appear even there during the time. One may enter a thicket safely where two would be heard."

"As you wish, *Tulku*," Magga said. She arose and went to the door. "*Mchog*

*Through the influence of one of the doctors in the case of Babies For Sale, several Los Angeles newspapers ran stories on a person known as the Green Lama trying to break into The Sanctuary Hospital to steal drugs. These stories were never retracted.

gi dnos grub,*" she said softly—and was gone.

IT LACKED twenty minutes of two o'clock in the morning when the Green Lama's cabin door opened and he stepped silently into the foyer. The ship was silent and only a slight quiver underfoot told that they were moving. Seeming to blend with the very shadows in the foyer, the Green Lama walked through the lounge and out onto the promenade deck. There he made his way toward the bridge.

The stars were brilliant and there was a three-quarters moon overhead, making the promenade deck almost ghostly in appearance. As from a great distance he could hear the slight swish of the water as the liner cut its way southward through the Pacific. Far ahead of him on the bridge the Green Lama saw a moving figure, the moonlight glinting from brass buttons. It was the second mate.

The Green Lama moved slowly and carefully toward the bridge. According to the plans related by Magga, he still had at least fifteen minutes before the Mexican would arrive and he didn't want the second mate to glimpse him before then.

He was within twenty or thirty feet of the bridge when it happened. The officer had turned on his heel and was walking toward the bow, his back toward the Lama. A shadowy figure detached itself from a lifeboat and leaped toward the officer's back. The moonlight flashed on the weapon in his right hand.

Something was wrong! They were attacking earlier. The Green Lama sped swiftly across the intervening twenty feet, a silent prayer on his lips.

But he was too late! When he was

*"The excellent success."

Huge lights played on the small boat tossing on the waves

still a good eight feet away, the hand holding the knife plunged downward. There was a dull thud, a choked cough and the second mate dropped to the deck, kicking convulsively. Then he was still, the hilt of the knife sticking out of his back on the left side.

The Green Lama reached the killer, his right arm chopping down in a blow across the back of the man's skull. The slayer dropped to the deck beside his victim.

The Green Lama knelt on one knee and rolled the killer over. It was Lopez. He was completely unconscious and would be for some time. The Green Lama started to turn to the second mate to see if there was a spark of life left. As he did, he heard the soft scrape of leather against wood behind him, and then he remembered that Magga had told him that Shallet and Foran were to accompany Lopez. In the heat of trying to save the officer's life, he had forgotten that.

Whirling, the Green Lama leaped sideways. But for the second time that night, he was too late. He had a momentary glimpse of the big first mate standing almost on top of him and then Shallet's fist raked along his jaw with a jar. The Lama spun around and crumpled across Lopez. He was not completely out but his legs were numb and there was a singing in his head. Vaguely he was conscious of trying to rise and of the fact that his legs refused to obey. As though from a great distance he could hear Shallet and Foran talking.

"The meddling fool!" Foran said. "He almost ruined things. But it's just as well. We'll toss him overboard with Martin and they'll just think the Green Lama's pulled another of his spectacular escapes. Come on, grab a hold."

The two men, grunting, lifted the body of the second mate, took the few steps to the rail and with a couple of swings hove the body over. Then they came back and leaned over the green-robed figure. As they did, Foran put one hand on the chest of the man beneath.

"He didn't kill Lopez anyway," he grunted. "Okay." The two men grabbed the head and feet of the man in green and again walked to the rail. A couple of swings and the body arched over the railing, the green robe fluttering out like wings, and plummeted out of sight. The two men turned back to the bridge.

CHAPTER V

Escape Into Irons

AT THE time the Green Lama was in his stateroom, t w i r l i n g his prayer wheel, five people were g a t h e r e d around a table in suite A—and unknown to them, a sixth person was listening from the next room. Only one light burned in the room where the five sat, a small light hooded with a reflector and tilted away from the head of the table.

The rays of the light were concentrated on the table but enough of them reflected upward to illumine the faces of four of the five people sitting there. On one side was Lopez, the diminutive Mexican, half lost in a marijuana dream, a fixed smile on his face. His hands held a slender dagger-knife, his fingers stroking the slim blade. Next to him sat Terrill Foran, the tall, sandy-haired man who had sat next to Magga at the captain's table. He was the only one there who did not keep glancing with fear toward the head of the table.

Across from Foran and Lopez, sat Shallet, the, huge blond-headed first mate. He was obviously ill at ease, his big hands twisting together, beads of sweat glistening on his brow. Every few minutes he would look, from beneath lowered brows, at the shadowy figure at the head of the table. Next to him was the tall, gaunt Nord—the man with the death's head face. Even Nord, the impassive executioner, seemed nervous in the presence of the unknown.

The person who was the center of their half-veiled glances sat back from the table, out of the circle of light. The figure was heavily muffled in a coat, despite the warm temperature, and wore a slouch hat pulled well over the face. Only the hands, slender and pale yet giving an impression of strength, were in the light, resting on the table edge. On the third finger of the right hand was a huge silver and jade ring—a raised silver, inverted pentagram with a jade death's head in the center. The light flashed from the silver pentagram as the hands moved expressively.

"You say your second in command is suspicious of you?" the figure at the head of the table asked. At the sound of the voice the listener in the next room knew another reason why the men at the table were nervous. The person spoke in an eerie whisper—void of expression, soulless.

Shallet, to whom the question was addressed, nodded. "Yeah," he said. "He either saw me putting the box away, or saw enough to arouse his suspicions. He doesn't know what it is but suspects some kind of a racket. He's probably looking for a chance to cut in on some gravy himself and if he doesn't get it he will go to the old man."

"He would probably be satisfied with a little," Foran said. "Why not let Shallet slip him a couple hundred bucks to forget what he saw? Would that do the trick, Shallet?"

"I think so." The big mate nodded.

"No," the voice whispered. "We need no more men and a man bought is only yours until someone comes along and offers a higher price. He must be paid off in another way. . ."

"You mean killed?" Shallet asked, his face paling.

"Yes," the whisper said.

"Can't—can't we do it some other way?" the first mate asked. One big hand dabbed at the sweat on his brow.

"No," the unseen leader said. "There is too much at stake. Already trouble is brewing in New York although they haven't touched this end of it yet. I had a cablegram today and everything is set for nation-wide distribution. It means millions of dollars a year, to say nothing of the diamond business, even if this—" the left hand pointed towards the ring on the right—"is ended. No, this man who threatens that must die!"

"A murder of an officer, on top of our Mr. Walters, may throw a monkey wrench into the works too," Foran said. "Don't forget that the captain has already been warned that you are on board. He still thinks that a Mr. Walters committed suicide but another death may convince him there has been two murders and then he will really turn the ship upside down looking for you. Might it not be better to buy the second mate off until we reach port?"

"No search will ever find me," the whisperer said. "Besides I have a plan. The Green Lama."

"What about him?"

"Lopez is a good forger. He will forge a confession signed by the second mate. In it will be the complete plans of this master smuggler and of the murder of Mr. Walters and will name the head of the smugglers—the Green Lama. It will be the mate's suicide confession; overcome with remorse and

shame, he decides to end it all—but not before he names the man responsible for all his crimes."

"The only thing," Foran said, "is can we be sure that Dr. Pali is the Green Lama? Sure enough to go ahead with such a plan?"

"Yes," came the whisper. "I myself have watched him come out of his stateroom, wearing the long green robe. He will not be in a position to prove that he is not the head of the smuggling ring and the captain will have no other choice but put him in irons."

"It sounds all right," Foran said after a short hesitation.

"The second mate will be on the bridge at two o'clock in the morning, won't he?" the leader asked Shallet.

"Yes."

"Good. Lopez will come up behind him with his knife. Shallet and Foran will go along to see that the job is done. Later, Shallet can plant the forged note in the second mate's quarters. And—" the whisper grew even fainter, until the four men had to lean forward, until the listener in the next room could not hear—"since the Green Lama has a way of learning our plans, Foran and Shallet will hang behind in the shadows. Should the Green Lama try to interfere with the execution, you can let him follow the second mate. When the note is found it will look merely as though he had escaped. Also, go a few minutes early to the bridge in the event he expects you at two.

"You, Foran—" the whisper grew stronger—"will report to me afterwards in the usual manner. You understand what you have to do?"

Foran and Lopez nodded. Shallet twisted in his seat and then looked toward the head of the table. "I don't like it," he said. "Couldn't we handle it without murder?"

"You are not paid to like or dislike anything—or even to think," the voice whispered tonelessly. "When you start to do that you become dangerous. Do you understand what you are to do?"

"Yes," Shallet said, shivering slightly.

"What about me?" Nord asked, speaking for the first time.

"You will remain here," the voice said. "Should they fail, then it will be up to you. But they had better not fail. Does everyone understand his part?"

The three men nodded.

"See that you carry it out," the leader whispered. The hand wearing the ring went upward and pulled the light cord. The stateroom was plunged into darkness. The four men sat silently as they listened to the other move across the room. The door opened and closed. The head of the smuggling ring was gone.

IT LACKED several minutes of two in the morning when the three men left Suite A and went up on the top deck. Lopez went almost to the bridge and hid in the shadow of a lifeboat. His knife was gripped in his right hand. Shallet and Foran hung back and watched. The big mate's teeth were chattering.

Foran nudged Shallet with his elbow and pointed. Coming across the promenade deck, almost indistinguishable from the shadows, was a figure in a long, hooded robe.

"The Green Lama," whispered Foran. "The man is almost inhuman. How did he learn about this?"

"I don't like this," Shallet repeated stubbornly. "I don't—".

"Shut up," Foran whispered sharply.

They stood there and watched as the green-robed figure stole across the deck towards the bridge where Martin, the second mate, stood. There was a sharp intake of breath from Shallet as Lopez darted from the shadow of the lifeboat and hurled himself at Martin's back.

"Now!" Foran said, as the Green Lama sped after the Mexican. "He'll be concentrating on Lopez and we'll have a chance to be on him before he knows it." The two men went cautiously forward.

The slender blade of the knife had just sank between the shoulder blades of the second mate when the chopping blow of the Green Lama's hand sent Lopez to the deck beside his victim. The Green Lama bent over the mate.

Shallet, closing in on the Lama, suddenly felt better. This was something he understood better—direct action. His big fists curled and tightened. A few more quick steps and he was directly behind the man in green. His right arm drew back.

As though sensing his presence, the Green Lama straightened and whirled. The big first mate shifted his feet and lashed out with his right fist. It caught the Green Lama on the side of the jaw and he went down on top of Lopez.

"Good work," Foran said approvingly. "The meddling fool! He almost ruined things. But it's just as well. We'll toss him overboard with Martin and they'll just think he's pulled another of his spectacular escapes. Come on, grab a hold."

The two men bent down and grabbed the head and feet of the second mate. They carried him to the railing and tossed him over. Then they went back and bent over the green-robed figure. Foran reached down and felt the chest of the man lying under him. Then they picked up the man in green.

"Pretty light for a guy that looks as big as he does," Shallet said as they threw him overboard.

"Come on," Foran said. "We've got to get Lopez and get back to the—" He broke off with a curse as they came back to the empty bridge.

"Where the hell is Lopez? He certainly didn't come to that quick and walk off. Unless that blow plus the marijuana has sent him off his nut completely."

"You don't suppose . . ." began Shallet, getting frightened again now that the action was over. Whatever the thought that had occurred to him, it was evidently more than he cared to put in words.

"You fools!" a voice whispered from near by. The two men glanced around and saw a slight, muffled figure standing on the deck. It was the leader.

"You fools!" the voice repeated again. "You've just murdered Lopez!"

Even Foran was taken back by the venom in the whispering voice. "Impossible," he said. "We left Lopez lying on the deck right here while we went to throw the Green Lama overboard."

"That was Lopez in the green robe," the hoarse whisper continued. "If you'd had your wits about you, you would have known it was too light for a man as big as the Green Lama. Fools!"

"But where is the Green Lama then?"

"He can't be far. Look around."

"But how could it happen?" the bewildered Shallet said. "I knocked him out and he fell on top of Lopez. It took us only a minute to throw Martin overboard and he was still lying on top of Lopez."

"Obviously he was knocked out," the whispering voice said. "He must have had enough strength to put his robe on Lopez and then put Lopez on top of him. He can't be far. Quick, look for him!"

THE muffled leader had correctly guessed the action of the Green Lama. Again trying to get up when the two men had taken the body of the second mate, the Lama had found his legs too weak to hold him. His head was still ringing from the blow. He knew that he couldn't regain his strength before they returned yet he had to do something. He slipped out of his robe and managed to get it on the Mexican. Then he raised Lopez enough to crawl under him. He threw one arm carelessly over his face and waited.

When Shallet and Foran lifted the body of Lopez, attired in the green robe, the Lama crawled rapidly across the deck and into the shadow of a lifeboat. From there he heard the conversation of the two men with their leader. If it hadn't been for the appearance of that muffled figure he might have gotten away with it; the two men delayed looking for him long enough to have regained his strength. He had gambled and lost. He shrugged his shoulders and waited for them to find him. There was no point in trying to escape by crawling and his legs were still too paralyzed to carry him away.

And find him they did within a few seconds. With the muffled leader directing their search, the first place they looked was the lifeboat. Shallet was the first to see him and dragged him roughly out into the moonlight.

"By heaven, it is Father Pali," Foran exclaimed, as he caught sight of the Green Lama's face.

The Green Lama was silent, staring calmly back at the three in front of him.

"That was a nice lecture you gave on Buddhism the other night," Foran said.

"Would you like to show us how a good Buddhist prays before being tossed into the Pacific ocean?"

"It is not necessary," the Green Lama said quietly. "My prayers are said and I have long been familiar with the *Bardo Tôd Tol**. A man who is prepared to go and join his ancestors does not make prayers through fear."

"Okay," Foran said cheerfully. "Overboard with him, Shallet."

"Wait!" came the command in the hoarse whisper. The muffled figure moved closer, but still even the keen eyes of the Green Lama could not find enough of the face to identify.

"What is your game?" the whisperer asked. "Why do you bother us? Are you a hi-jacker?"

The Green Lama smiled. "You have nothing which I want," he said. "Rather do you stand for something which I do not want. I am only a part of the suffering which must follow you."

"What the hell's the guy talking about?" snapped Shallet.

"It is written in the Dhammapada," the Green Lama continued, "that the prime element in all is thought. Preponderant is thought, by thought all is made. If a man speak or act with evil thought, suffering follows him as the wheel follows the hoof of the beast that draws the cart. There is enough evil in the thoughts which you have concerning the small steel box to darken the sky of the universe."

"What do you know of the steel box?" the voice asked.

"Only what it contains and what is to be done with it, O One Who Walks in Darkness. If I don't stop it, others will."

"Let's stop this chatter," Foran said, "and toss him overboard."

* A Tibetan classic on the peregrinations of the dead in the next world.

"I have changed the plans," the whispering voice said. "Take him below and lock him in irons. You Shallet will discover the note in your second's quarters and will have arrested the Green Lama. Once he's locked up, you can so report to your captain. Do it now." The muffled figure turned and walked briskly towards the promenade deck.

With the Green Lama between them, Shallet and Foran went aft until they came to the stairway at the end of the small ballroom. Keeping a careful watch, they descended down past the three decks into the hold. The Green Lama, a calm smile on his face, made no attempt to get away.

Once in the hold, the big first mate led the way to two small cells in the stern. One of these he unlocked with a key from his pocket and they shoved the Green Lama in. Shallet followed after him and very deliberately searched him, taking everything that was in the Green Lama's pockets and even removing the small prayer wheel from around his neck. He handed everything out to Foran.

"Maybe there ain't nothing there he could pick a lock with and maybe there is," he said.

"A good idea," Foran said.

Shallet picked up heavy leg-irons and handcuffs from the floor and quickly cuffed the Green Lama. Chains ran from the leg-irons to the wall.

"Guess that'll hold him," the first mate remarked. He backed out of the cell and locked the door. The two men turned toward the stairs.

"Good night, Father," Foran called lightly as they started up.

Back of the two men, a whisper floated after them, clear above the pulsing of the ship's engines: *"Om! Ma-ni pad-me Hum!"*

CHAPTER VI

Charged With Murder

 ARY BROWN and Evangl Stewart were waiting on the deck of the *S. S. Cathay* when she docked at eight o'clock in the morning at Balboa on the Pacific end of the Panama Canal. They had gotten up early and had breakfasted so that they could get off as soon as the boat docked. They would only be there for five hours and they wanted to take full advantage of it. Several others evidently had the same idea for the deck was crowded with passengers waiting for the gang-plank to be lowered. Standing close to them were Jean Farrell, the good-looking young redhead, and Ken Clayton, the actor. Jean caught sight of Evangl and waved.

"Hi-ho,' she called. "Off to the land of Panama hats and sun-burned soldiers. What say we ditch the boy friends and grab a marine as soon as we get ashore?"

"Not a chance," Gary said emphatically. Evangl laughed as though to say: You see how it is.

"Men!" the redhead said scornfully. "You've got that big lug ordering you around and here I am with a handsome Rollo trying to slap me over with that fatal Hollywood charm. He even has to wait for someone to yell 'Camera! Lights! Action!' before he can go into a clinch."

The good-looking actor grinned and winked at Gary as he steered the redhead toward the gangplank. Just ahead of them was the talkative Mrs. Forbes with another woman.

"Where's your friend, the Buddhist," Jean Farrell called back to Gary and Evangl.

"Haven't seen him this morning," Evangl said.

"Maybe he's got a little dyspepsia, Jean said. "I saw him leaving his stateroom last night looking as if he were dressed for a masquerade. But maybe

Carlos Lopez

that's the kind of nightshirts they wear in Tibet."

Gary and Evangl exchanged looks at this but said nothing. They followed the others down the gangplank. As they left the deck, they passed the captain standing by the rail. With him was the big first mate, Shallet.

"The captain looks mad about something," Gary said. "I wonder if the Green Lama's been up to something and the captain's in a stew because he can't find out what's going on?"

"Probably Captain Betts just hates to have to get up so early in the morning," Evangl said.

"You know it is funny," Gary went on, looking back at the ship, "but neither the Green Lama nor Dr. Valco

is around this morning. And I don't
see anything of that rat, Lopez, either."

"Stop trying to build up a mystery,"
Evangl said. "Come on. You've got to
take me to Panama City shopping."
Reluctantly, Gary let her pull him over
to a cab.

IT WAS about twenty minutes before
sailing time when Gary and Evangl
arrived back on the ship, loaded down
with the souvenirs and gifts that she
had bought. They put their things away
in their staterooms and went down on
Deck C for lunch. While they were
eating, they felt the steamer get under
way again.

They were about half way through
lunch when Senorita Carmen Esteban
entered the dining room. Spotting them,
she made for their table.

"Here comes that Spanish dame,"
Gary muttered under his breath.

"Well," Evangl said, "just see that
you get no yen for the South American
Way, or I'll scratch her eyes out."

"Oh, you can't take it, huh? I noticed you thought it was funny when
I didn't like the idea of that Jethro
Dumont guy hanging around you and
now—"

"Shh," Evangl said, pinching his
arm playfully.

"Do I interrupt a lovers' quarrel?"
the senorita asked as she came up to
the table. She pulled out the extra chair
and sat down.

"Won't you join us?" Evangl asked
sweetly.

Their visitor grinned. "It is written,"
she said, "that people in love are im-
prisoned within themselves: *Gyab rii
tag, Dun rii tso**."

"You—" Gary began questioningly,
leaning forward.

"*Nimitta; nibbana, lobha, dosa,
moha**," she said softly.

"Magga," Evangl exclaimed. "Why
didn't you let us know before?"

"It wasn't necessary before," Magga
said.

"The Green Lama is in trouble?"
Gary asked.

"Yes. He is under arrest, charged
with the murder of Mr. Walters, Second Mate Martin and Senor Carlos
Lopez."

"What?" Gary exclaimed.

"Martin and Lopez vanished last
night," Magga said. "A note was found,
by First Mate Shallet, in Martin's quarters naming the Green Lama as the
head of the smuggling ring who the
captain was warned was on board. The
first mate immediately arrested the
Green Lama and locked him up."

"Where is he?" Gary asked.

"Down in the hold," Magga said.

"Okay," Gary said grimly. He rose
from the table and started across the
dining room.

"Gary!" Evangl cried. "Wait—"

"Let him go," Magga said, putting
her hand on Evangl's arm. "You need
not worry about him. He'll take care
of himself."

Gary walked out of the dining room
and went up the stairs to his own stateroom. He yanked out a dresser drawer
and took from it the shoulder holster
and the automatic. He flung off his
coat and strapped on the holster. He
threw a shell in the barrel of the automatic, slipped it into the holster and
put on his coat. Then in the same de-
liberate fashion he walked out of the
cabin and started back down stairs.

Down in the hold, he saw the grilled
doors of the two cells at the one end.

* A quote from an old Tibetan poem. It means "The mountain rock behind, the mountain lake in front."

* This was the code used by the Green Lama when calling Gary over his short-wave radio from the Park Avenue headquarters in New York. It means, "The signs; ex-tinguish the fires of greed, ill will and ignorance."

No one guarded them. He walked over and looked in the first one. It was empty. Then he moved on to the next one. It too was empty! Leg-irons and handcuffs lay on the floor.

On the wall there was a rough chalk drawing of a Tibetan gargoyle and under it the symbol of *Om*. The Green Lama had escaped.

Gary turned and started back upstairs. The grimness was gone from his face, but he was still trying to think where to look for the Green Lama. He felt guilty about his neglect of his duty. But he and Evangl had been having so much fun that he hadn't thought that the Green Lama might be in danger.

He was on the stairway between Deck B and Deck A when he met Ken Clayton coming down. He nodded and started to push by when Clayton stopped him.

"We've never been introduced, so I'm not sure who you are," the actor said, "but I'll take a guess. Gary Brown?"

"Yeah," Gary said suspiciously. "So what?"

"The Green Lama asked me to find you and bring you to him," the actor said.

"What is this—a gag?" Gary demanded harshly, his right hand slipping toward his shoulder.

"No," Clayton said, grinning. "I was passing a door downstairs when someone called my name. It was Dr. Pali and he told me to hunt you up and tell you the Green Lama wants you."

"If this is a trap," Gary said, still suspicious, "you'll be the first one to get it."

"It's no trap," Clayton said. "I might mention many reasons why, but I'll tell you one. About the only friends I had in Hollywood were James Sandor and Bette Hall*. Does that explain it?"

"Maybe," Gary said. "You lead the way and I'll follow. If it's a trap, remember what I told you."

The good-looking actor smiled and led the way down the stairs.

SHORTLY after Foran and Shallet had left the night before, the Green Lama had gone to work. He raised his manacled hands and from the back of his collar he drew a tiny sliver of steel. It was so thin that, when it was in the collar, it followed the collar line without causing the slightest wrinkle or indication of its presence. The end of the pick slid into the keyhole on the handcuffs and a second later the cuffs sprang open. Then he bent over and went to work on the leg-irons. They were a little tougher but in less than two minutes they fell from his ankles. From the cuff of his trousers, he took a small piece of chalk and sketched a Tibetan gargoyle on the wall of the cell. Under it he put the symbol of *Om*.

Next he tackled the cell door. It too gave way before the steel pick and swung open. The Green Lama stepped out and swung the door closed. Smiling, he bent over with the pick and locked the door once more. He turned toward the stairs. It had taken him less than five minutes to escape from the cuffs and the cell**.

As he went up the stairs, his mind was busy with the problem of the next move. He couldn't return to his stateroom since, he knew, by this time Shallet would have convinced the captain that Dr. Pali, the Green Lama and the

* He was referring to the couple, in the case of *Babies For Sale*, who adopted a baby which, the Green Lama later proved, was their own baby kidnapped by the adoption syndicate a year before.
** According to some notes in one of the monographs in my possession, the Green Lama had once studied locks under Henri Croisson, once with the *Sûreté* in Paris and said to have been the greatest locksmith alive. Croisson died in June of 1939, however, so this cannot be verified.

head of the smuggling ring were all the same person. That, he had to admit, had been a clever move on the part of the unknown leader. With Captain Betts, who was the law as long as they were on the ship, against him, his movements were restricted considerably.

Reaching Deck C, he began to explore the end opposite the dining room. He had to find a place to hide before morning, and this deck seemed the most likely.

For a moment he considered the several storage rooms at the stern of the deck but finally decided that the risk of discovery was too great there. Then at the far end of the deck, he discovered the place. Right next to the hospital was the baggage room. The officers would have no occasion to enter it until New York was reached, unless an emergency required it. The door was locked but it was only a matter of seconds for the Green Lama to open it.

He entered and closed the door. A brief search in the dark turned up a couple of duffle bags which would make good pillows and shortly, the Green Lama had dropped off to sleep.

WHEN he awoke it was to feel the jerk of the boat docking at Balboa. He reasoned that most of the passengers would be going ashore for a few hours and that it would probably be impossible to get in touch with anyone until they returned. So he promptly went back to sleep.

Fully, rested, the Green Lama had been awake some time but made no move until he felt the steamer once more getting under way. Then he unlocked the door to the baggage room and opened it a fraction of an inch. Peering into the corridor through that small aperture, he patiently sat down to the long watch for someone he could

trust. One might not come at all; in which case he would have to wait until late that night.

It was perhaps an hour later when he saw Ken Clayton, the actor, pass and turn into the hospital door. In about fifteen minutes he was back, a small white bandage on one finger. The Green Lama whispered his name as he reached the baggage room.

Ken Clayton had not been making and idle boast when he said he was a good actor. It must have been quite a shock to hear a strange, eerie voice suddenly whisper his name from what was marked the baggage room. But his expression gave no indication of having heard anything. He merely stopped in front of the door and began a fruitless search through his pockets for a cigarette.

"Yes?" he asked quietly.

"This is Dr. Pali," the Green Lama said.

"I thought as much," Clayton said. "I overheard a couple of the officers talking about your arrest, and I could think of no one else who might be hiding in the baggage room."

The Green Lama chuckled softly. "Is there anyone around who can see you?" he asked.

"No."

"Good. You don't mind doing a service for me?"

"Not at all."

"Find Gary Brown for me. Do you know him?"

"I don't believe so," Ken said.

The Green Lama quickly described Gary and Clayton nodded. "I think I know who you mean," he said, "although I didn't know his name."

"Find him," the Green Lama continued, "and bring him down here to me. He may be a little hard-headed about it so tell him that the Green

Lama wants him." As he disclosed his identity, he watched the actor closely But Clayton only nodded.

"You are not surprised that I am the Green Lama?"

"No," Ken said. "I had already guessed it."

"And you're willing to help the heathen 'priest' who is supposed to be a smuggler and a murderer?" the Green Lama asked, a little surprised.

"I don't believe everything I hear," Ken said. He had at last succeeded in finding a cigarette and was now carrying on the same fruitless search for a match. "You see, I started on the inside track. Bette Hall and her husband were good friends of mine."

"I see," the Green Lama said. "It is truly written that one often looks at the mountain without seeing what is on it. You will bring Gary?"

"You bet," Clayton said. Finding a match, he lit his cigarette and strolled on.

WITHIN a few minutes he and Gary were back. "No one in sight," Ken Clayton reported quietly, without looking at the door.

The Green Lama swung the door open. "Come in quickly—both of you," he said. Gary and Ken stepped in and he closed the door. They were in complete darkness.

"I feel like a heel, chief," Gary said. "I should have been around more I guess but—"

"The man in love has eyes only in his heart," the Green Lama said. "It should not be otherwise. Do not flagellate yourself for an imagined carelessness. You could not have helped even if you had been there. But now there are a few things you can do. What time do we dock at Cristobal?"

"Sometime tonight," Gary said.

"Eight o'clock," Ken put in.

"And now it is—?"

"About two-thirty or three o'clock," Ken said. "I think we have already passed through the Miraflores Locks and are probably in the Pedro Miguel.

The Green Lama

Locks. About another five hours before we reach Limon Bay at Cristobal."

"We lay over there all night, don't we?" the Lama asked.

"Until seven in the morning," Clayton answered.

"When we reach Cristobal," the Green Lama said, "I think our friends Foran, Nord and Shallet will go ashore —as will probably many others. But those three will have a definite destination. I want you and Evangl to follow them, Gary. Don't try to get too close or to catch them. Just find out where they go."

"Okay," Gary said.

"How about me?" demanded Ken Clayton. "I want to get in on this too."

"Are you sure?" the Green Lama asked. "It may be dangerous."

"So what?" Clayton said.

"All right," the Green Lama said. "You can watch for another passenger who will go to the same place. It may be a man or a woman, or even a friend of yours. You must be suspicious of everyone. I imagine they will go somewhere in the native quarter of Colon. I'll help you both watch."

"But how'll you get off the ship?" Clayton asked.

"I'll get off," the Green Lama promised with a smile. "In the meantime, Gary, go up to my stateroom and get one of my robes out of my large suitcase. Bring it down to me."

"Okay, chief," Gary said. "You want me to bring you something to eat, too?"

"Better not. It might be dangerous. I've been eating too much since my return to America anyway. Just get the robe. And there's something else either, or both, of you can do. Find out if you can who on board has been sending a number of cablegrams to New York. Now go."

The Green Lama inched the door open and glanced into the hall. There was no one in sight. Gary and Ken slipped out and started down the corridor.

CHAPTER VII

A Night In Colon

 DARKNESS had already fallen on Cristobal when the *S. S. Cathay* stuck her long white nose through the waters of Limon Bay and edged up to the dock. The few streets that comprised the American part of the city, were well lighted, with neon signs blazing above the night clubs. At regular intervals two soldiers, or two sailors, would march along the street, looking into the night clubs as they passed. These were the police of Cristobal—Military Police or sailors from the Shore Patrol. It was impressive to watch the two uniformed men marching along abreast, their clubs swinging in time to their steps.

Gary Brown and Evangl stood on the deck and watched the gangplank lowered. A few passengers were already waiting to go ashore and these hurried off the boat and headed for the night clubs. A few feet away from Gary and Evangl, Ken Clayton was standing with Jean Farrell. Ken said something to her in an undertone and came over to Gary.

"What the hell am I going to do?" he asked. "She's insisting that I take her through the native quarter of Colon and says she'll go by herself if I don't. I don't know whether I should stay and watch for someone else or go with her. When I checked up on that cablegram business this afternoon, she was one of the four who has been sending a lot. It'll be just my luck to find a girl that I like only to discover she's a female ogre."

"Go ahead and go with her," Gary said.

"What are you lugs plotting now?" Jean asked, moving over to join them. "When two good-looking guys like that get their heads together, it bodes no good for us gals," she said to Evangl.

Evangl laughed. "If Gary tries any plotting," she said, "I'll walk all over him."

"You hear that?" the redhead said to Ken. "She's got the right idea. Now do you take me to Colon or do I start walking all over you?"

"Ah, you young people," a voice said behind them. All four turned around and saw Mrs. Maryland Forbes beaming at them.

"That's all you need when you're in love," she said, "a boat and a tropic moon. I know. My husband and I took a trip to Bermuda on our honeymoon and it was simply wonderful. Ever since then the poor dear's had to work so hard I always have to take my trips alone. But then he's so tickled to see me when I get back home, I believe it's worth it." She beamed at them again and walked down the gangplank and towards one of the night clubs.

"There goes one of the biggest arguments against matrimony I've ever seen," Ken Clayton said.

"So who's talking matrimony?" Jean said. "I'll settle for Colon. Come on, Romeo." She seized him by the arm and the two of them walked off the ship and hailed a cab. For a moment the deck was deserted.

Gary and Evangl were silent for a moment. Then Gary reached down and patted her hand. "Love me?" he asked.

"Do I!" she said, smiling tenderly at him.

"I'm crazy about you, darling," he said. "There's only one thing worries me—what's your mother going to say when she learns you're going to marry an ex-gangster?"

"Don't worry about mother," Evangl said. "Dad'll be on our side. And maybe we'll get some help from Jethro Dumont. If he puts in a good word, that'll fix her."

"That guy!" snorted Gary. "I won't—"

"Shh," Evangl said. "Here they come."

Terrill Foran and James Nord came along the deck to the gangplank.

"Not seeing the Panamanian sights?" Foran asked as they came abreast of the couple

"Maybe later," Gary said.

"They're worth seeing, even if you have to skip a moon," Foran said, laughing. He went on down the gangplank followed by the man with the death's head face.

"Come on," Evangl whispered.

"Not yet," Gary whispered back. "There's still Shallet."

In another minute the big first mate came on deck dressed in his shore uniform. He passed Gary and Evangl without saying a word and went off in the same direction taken by Foran and Nord. A little later, Gary and Evangl followed.

They had been gone but a few minutes when a shadowy, hooded figure came on deck and silently went ashore.

A MINUTE later a half-drowsing cab driver was aroused by a voice speaking from the back seat of his cab. He had heard no one approach nor had he heard the door of his cab open and shut. Little wonder then that he started at the sound of the voice and crossed himself hurriedly.

"Take me over to the native section of Colon," the voice said in Spanish. "If you overtake other cabs with passengers from the ship, it might be wise to follow them. That way we can see where is the best place to go."

"Si, Senor," the driver said and started his old car. It moved ahead with a jerk and then began careening towards Colon, the Panamanian side of the city.

As they entered the native quarter, they caught up with two other cabs. The Green Lama's—for it was he—driver fell in behind them. But evidently he fidgeted at the slow pace. He twisted half around in his seat.

"If the *Senor* is looking for some native dancing girls or would care to risk a few *balboas** at a game of chance—"

"I don't," the Green Lama interrupted. "Wherever the others are going is good enough for me."

"As you desire, *Senor*," the driver said, shrugging.

The first cab suddenly pulled over to the curb and stopped before a small native store. The second cab, in which Gary and Evangel were riding, pulled past it and drove slowly on down the street. At the next corner it turned to the right.

The Green Lama's driver, told to follow both cabs and faced with the necessity of choosing one, wavered for a minute and then swerved sharply to the curb, pulling up behind the other cab with screeching brakes. In fact his decision was so late he almost collided with the car he had chosen.

As soon as he saw everything was under control, he turned to his passenger. "If you had but told me, *Senor*—" he began. Then he broke off with a gasp.

There was no one sitting in the back seat of his cab. But on the seat there were two American dollars. The driver grabbed them with one hand while he crossed himself with the other. "*Dios*," he muttered for his spiritual side while his practical side saw to the putting away of the money.

Attracted by the squealing brakes directly behind them, Foran, Nord and Shallet, who had already alighted and paid their bill, came back to the cab. They peered in but saw no one but the driver.

"What's the meaning of this?" demanded Shallet in Spanish. He was get-

* A Panamanian monetary unit, worth approximately $1.00. American money, however, is usually accepted anywhere in Panama.

ting nervous and irritable again. "You almost struck us."

"*Senor*," the driver said, "I am an imbecile. Perhaps my mother drop me on my head. But I am driving alone, thinking I have a passenger, and then I am almost run into your cab. I stop quick like the lightning and turn to my passenger." The driver shrugged and grinned. "But my passenger—he is not."

"He's just been smoking too much loco weed," Foran said. He threw back his head and laughed loudly. Shallet laughed nervously and even Nord managed what passed for a grin. The driver at the sight of the grinning death's head crossed himself for the third time and drove hurriedly off, so upset that he went straight home instead of looking for more business. The three men turned and entered the shop.

WHEN he saw that his cab was pulling directly in behind the cab ahead, and doing it obviously, the Green Lama jerked two dollars out of his pocket and threw it on the seat. As the cab skidded to a stop, he opened the door and stepped out. By the time the driver had looked around, the Green Lama was in the shadow of the building next to the shop.

The Green Lama waited in the shadows for several minutes and then slipped down the street past the front of the store. There was no one inside but the shopkeeper, leaning against a counter piled high with Panama hats of all shapes.

Deciding that that must mean there was a meeting place in the rear of the shop, the Green Lama made up his mind to enter. He threw the hood of his robe back on his shoulders so that the shopkeeper wouldn't be too suspicious in the beginning. With the hood back and his ecclesiastical collar show-ing, he would look enough like a visit-ing monk to get into the shop. He walked boldly in through the front en-trance.

"Have you any rosary beads?" he asked in Spanish.

"But yes, *padre*," the shopkeeper said, "Many of them. You have but to—"

His speech shut off abruptly in the middle. The Green Lama had arrived within reaching distance and his right hand flashed out and pressed on the back of the man's skull*. The shop-keeper crumpled to the floor. He would be out for at least an hour.

Adjusting his hood once more over his face, the Green Lama walked to the back of the room, leaving the shop-keeper lying behind the counter out of sight. There was a curtain over a door-way in the back. He stopped at this and listened for a moment. He could hear the slight drone of voices as though from a distance. He stepped through the curtain and found himself in a dark hallway. Ahead of him a glimmer of light streamed from an open door.

Silently, the Green Lama slipped down the hall until he stood beside the door. A quick glance within revealed Foran, Nord and Shallet sitting at a large table. Three other men were at the table with them; two natives and a third man who appeared to be an American. They were all bent over something on the table.

While their attention was centered on the table, the Green Lama slipped past the doorway so that he stood on the far side of the room. Once more he glanced around the doorsill.

"But, *Senor*, this is the best," one of the natives was protesting.

<hr/>

* Although there was no mention of it in this monograph, the Green Lama had obviously made himself radioactive before leaving the ship. Otherwise a blow would have been necessary and, according to the record, in this case he merely pressed lightly on the *medulla oblongata*.

"I don't agree with you," Foran said. "It's not as good as the last batch you supplied us with. So we are paying you three dollars an ounce less."

"But, *Senor*—" began the native again.

Ken Clayton

"Shut up, Pedro," the American said. He leaned across the table. "What's the racket, Foran? You know as well as I do that this is the same grade as before. So what's it mean? You suddenly got the market sewed up, or something?"

"SOMETHING like that," Foran admitted. "We've got the market sewed up enough to see to it that you don't sell to any one else—at least not more than once. But we'll be using five or six times as much as before. So the boss says we get a wholesale price—three dollars less on the ounce—or else . . ."

"So it's like that, eh?" the American said. "I thought maybe it was comin'. Say, Foran, who the hell is this boss of yours anyway? The last time he comes around here muffled up like the bandit in a horse opera and now suddenly he's got the market all done up in a little bag. Who is he?"

"That is not necessary for you to know," Foran said shortly. "The question is, do we get it at the new price?"

"You get it," the American said. "What the hell am I going to do—cut my own throat? You'll cut it quick enough for me without me doing the job myself. Where's the dough?"

"Here," Foran said. He brought a package of American money out of his pocket and put it on the table. The American picked it up and counted it hurriedly.

"Okay," he said. "It's all yours." He nodded at the box on the table. The Green Lama could see it was filled with small packages. A couple of the packages were on the table, opened. They were filled with a white substance, somewhat similar to sugar in appearance. But the Green Lama recognized it for what it was—cocaine.

"Don't forget," Foran was saying as he picked up the box, "we want about six times as much on the next trip."

"Okay," the American said. "We'll have it for you. How the hell are you gonna get rid of all that, Foran?"

"The syndicate," Foran said, "is going to start putting it out at high schools all over the country. We're cutting out all the marijuana peddling at those sources. The weed's too easy to get, or they can even grow it themselves, so the price is chiseled down too low. Give them snow and we can keep the price up because they can't buy it anywhere else."

"Kids, huh?" the American grunted. "We certainly do a dirty job when we go to work, don't we, Foran?"

"If you don't like it, you can always get out," Foran said.

"Oh I like it—or at least the dough I get out of it. And I don't like the only way there is to get out. How you going to handle the sales?"

"Straight to the kids," Foran said. "We're gonna send guys out peddling these comic magazines. They'll all be the regular magazines only there'll be something extra in them. And they'll sell for a special price. That's the boss' idea."

"Pretty slick," the American said. "Working it from both ends?"

"Yeah. New York and L.A."

"When'll you be through again?"

"In two weeks, on the return trip," Foran said. "Only it'll probably be Max. I may not come through at all after this. And after while, Shallet here may handle all the pick-ups. I'm going to handle the New York end."

"Getting to be a big shot, eh?"

"Sort of. Looks like the ring in New York is folding up, with everyone getting on the sing-wagon, so we've got to build this angle of it up. That's one place the boss is smart; always moving one step ahead of the cops."

"Yeah, and keeping us just one step ahead of starvation with the prices," grunted the American.

"You'll get along," Foran said, smiling. He picked up the box and got up from the table. "Let's go," he added to Nord and Shallet. The three of them moved toward the door.

CHAPTER VIII

Hold The Boat

FOR a minute the Green Lama was undecided what to do. He felt confident that once the three men stepped into the dark hallway, he could knock out all three and still get into

the room and capture the others. But of still more importance was the capture of the leader. And if he took the three from the boat now, he might not get another lead to the boss for some time. So he stood motionless in the shadows and let the men walk down the hallway and vanish through the curtain. Then he turned back to the room.

". . . I'm afraid that's the way it is, *amigos*," the American was saying. "When you get a syndicate like that, they play for keeps. We either take the price they offer us or we get our throats slit some fine night and they find someone else who will take that price—especially when they are reminded about what happened to us. Sometimes I think we'd make more money being honest. It's getting so crime don't pay unless you're sitting at the head of the table."

"We could perhaps steal after them and *point* out the injustice of it," the one called Pedro suggested softly, his hand toying with the knife at his belt.

"No," the American said, shaking his head. "That would only make it worse. Don't forget that they have—" He broke off to stare at the figure that stood in the doorway, watching them. It was a tall figure, garbed in a dark green hooded robe.

"What the hell is this—a masquerade?" the American demanded.

"Hardly," the Green Lama said quietly. "To your friends who have just left I am known as the Green Lama. In Tibet there is a proverb that says the man who walks in darkness must expect to stumble over a rock. I am that rock."

"Like that, huh?" the American said, his eyes narrowing. He snapped something in Spanish and grabbed for the gun in his pocket. But he never reached it.

The Green Lama flashed across the room, pulling the red *kata* from around his neck. Just as the American's gun was clearing the top of his pocket, the scarf looped out and fell around his neck. The Green Lama twisted and jerked slightly. The American fell forward, unconscious. A harder jerk and he would have been dead but as it was he would be out for a couple of hours.

As the Green Lama whirled around, the two Panamanians were coming in at him from both sides, drawn knives in their hands. The Green Lama flashed in to meet them, moving to one side to bring one of them closer. As they came together, the first native slashed upward with his knife. The Green Lama grabbed the native's wrist, when the knife was less than an inch away, and twisted. His other hand darted down and grabbed the man by the leg. The knife clattered to the floor and the surprised native found himself hurtling into his companion. They both crashed to the floor.

They had hardly struck when the Green Lama was over them. His hands reached down and quickly pressed the nerves at the back of their skulls. The natives relaxed.

Listening intently until he was sure there was no one else in the house, the Green Lama turned and left the room. As he pushed aside the curtain and entered the front shop, the dark hallway seemed to be filled with a lingering echo, unheard by the unconscious men, *"Om! Ma-ni pad-me Hum!"*

OUTSIDE, the Green Lama explored the block but saw nothing of Gary and Evangl or of their cab. Deciding that they must have returned to the ship, the Green Lama started back for the American quarter of the town.

Crossing the boundary line into Cristobal, the Green Lama walked toward two M.P.s coming along the street. He had thrown the hood of his robe back again, and the ecclesiastical collar showed at the throat. He stopped in front of the soldiers.

"Good evening, soldiers," he said.

"Good evening, Father," the men replied. They were a little puzzled by the color of the monk's robe but felt reassured by the sight of the collar.

"Do the Colon police coöperate with you?" the Green Lama asked.

"Sometimes," one the the soldiers said, "and sometimes we just go in and help ourselves. What's the matter, Father?"

"You know where the Sebastian shop is on Guipuzcoa Street?"

"Yeah."

"In the back room there you will find three men who peddle cocaine. The man in front is in with them. I expect you may find some cocaine on them and on the American you will find the money he just received for a sale. They are unconscious but will recover within one to two hours."

As he finished talking, the Green Lama moved around the two astonished soldiers and started walking rapidly away. As he went, he pulled the hood over his head. In a few steps he had reached a shadowy side of the street.

"Hey, wait!" yelled one of the soldiers. "Who the hell are you?" There was no answer and he yanked on the pistol at his hip. "Halt, or I'll fire . . . Now, where the hell did he go?" The two soldiers were staring at an apparently deserted street.

Back on the boat, the Green Lama slipped down to Deck B and stopped outside of Suite A. Inside he could hear Nord and Foran talking but evidently there was no one else with them. They would probably report to their leader in the morning. The Green Lama turned and went back up to his stateroom on Deck A. A few minutes later he was asleep.

IT MUST have been about four in the morning when the Green Lama was aroused by someone knocking lightly at his door. Expecting to go back down to the baggage room before daylight, he had gone to sleep fully clothed except for his green robe. Now he jumped up and slipped it on. If it were the captain at the door and he had to escape he wanted the robe.

He went to the door and put his hand on the knob. "Who's there?" he asked.

"Magga," came the muffled answer from the other side. He swung the door open and she came in.

Her hair and dress were disheveled and there were raw, red marks over her wrists. She was evidently exhausted.

"They've got Gary and Evangl," she said as soon as she was in the room.

"Who?" the Green Lama asked, tensely.

"Some part of the gang in Colon," Magga said. She sat down on the edge of the bed. "When you left," she continued, "I decided to follow you. I was in another cab quite a distance behind yours. When your cab pulled in behind the other in front of that little shop, I went on down the street and left mine several blocks away. I walked back towards the shop and when I was fairly close I stopped across the street and watched. I saw you enter the shop.

"A little later, a muffled figure came out of the house next to the shop and hurried down the side street. I thought it was the head of the smugglers from the boat and was about to follow when Gary and Evangl came around the corner of the street opposite me; on the same side as the shop. They had evidently seen you stop there and were going to try to sneak up and be of some help. As they came abreast of the house next door, a man came down the steps and stopped them. They stood there for a few seconds and then the three of them walked back into the house. Gary was walking very stiffly as though someone had a gun on him.

"I did some fast thinking and decided that muffled figure had been the boss who somehow had known that Gary and Evangl were following the men. It had been arranged to capture them.

"So instead of trying to follow the leader, I went across to the house, found a loose window and got inside. And I didn't more than straighten up when someone grabbed me. They took me upstairs and put me in a room by myself. But as we went along the hall, I caught a glimpse of Gary and Evangl being tied up in another room.

"They did a good job of tying me

The body arched over the railing, the green robe fluttering out, and plummeted down toward the water and it took me until now to get loose. You've got to do something, *Tulku!* I think they're going to kill them!"

"I'll go immediately," the Green Lama said. "You better get into your stateroom and get some rest."

"I am a mess," Magga said. "The sailor at the gangplank almost didn't let me on board. *Tulku*, you will get them?" She put one hand on his arm.

"Yes, *Jetsunma*," he said gently. "Go and rest."

"If you're late," Magga said, "I'll hold the boat some way, even if I have to kidnap the captain. May Buddha guide your footsteps!"

"*Om vajra sattva!*" the Green Lama said. He left the stateroom and made his way through the lounge and out onto the promenade deck.

The sailor at the gangplank was bored and slightly sleepy, gazing out at the reflection of the moon on the bay. He was completely unaware of the shadowy figure that went silently by him and hurried toward Colon.

The little shop was closed and on the front door there was a huge padlock. The police had evidently been there, taken their prisoners and locked the store. The house next to it was dark, with no sign of life. The Green Lama stood on the deserted street for a moment, fingering the small prayer wheel at his neck. Then he made for the front door.

IT WAS only a matter of seconds and the tiny sliver of steel before the front door swung silently open. The Green Lama slipped into the hall.

From somewhere up the stairs he could hear the murmur of voices. He felt his way to the staircase and started up. The voices grew louder.

Once in the upper hallway, he could see a path of light where a door stood open. It was from there the voices were coming. Silently, the Green Lama went along the hall until he stood at the very edge of the door. He glanced around the edge of the sill, risking the chance of being seen.

Gary and Evangl were seated on two straight-backed chairs placed close together. They were both bound to the chairs and there were gags in their mouths. The only light in the room was a standing lamp, made like a searchlight and directed at the two in the chairs, leaving at least half the room in semi-darkness. Directly in front of them stood two men. One of them was holding a long knife in his right hand. In the dark side of the room another figure, heavily muffled, stood. It was this figure who was talking, in an unemotional whisper, as the Green Lama looked in. Occasionally the hands would move and the light would reflect from the silver and jade surface of a ring on the right hand.

". . . no, we shall not kill them," the voice was whispering, "this time. I have a better idea. First the man: you will cut off his ears. Later, we will send the ears to the Green Lama—if he is still alive. And the girl, with the so pretty face: On each cheek you will carve with the knife the design on my ring. You, Pablo, will revive her if she faints. Then when that is finished we will send them both as presents to the Green Lama on board the ship, to remind him not to bother us."

"Why send them?" the Green Lama spoke from the doorway. "The Green Lama comes to collect his presents himself."

At the sound of the voice, the two men whirled toward the doorway. The second man's hand went into his blouse and came out gripping a knife.

"That's him!" the whispering voice

said, almost breaking with emotion. "Pablo, Juan—get him!"

The two men moved cautiously forward obeying the order, their eyes glittering feverishly as they watched the Green Lama.

"*Om vajra guru pad-me siddhi Hum!*" the Green Lama chanted under his breath and came into the room with a rush.

He met the bigger of the two natives first, side-stepped the slashing blow of the long knife and the fingertips of his right hand stabbed beside the man's ear. With a howl of fear, the native went to the floor, his arms and legs threshing wildly*.

Almost with the same movement, the Green Lama kicked out with his right foot, landing on the shin of the other native. The force of the blow, plus the pain, sent him spinning half around, off balance, his knife slashing at empty air. Before he could regain his balance the Green Lama stepped in closer and brought the edge of his hand down at the base of his skull. The native fell, unconscious.

Again the Green Lama whirled, this time towards the darkened part of the room. But even as he leaped forward he saw that there was no one there.

---

*He had struck the vestibular nerve (Cranial VIII) which controls the equilibrium. Although the native was fully conscious, he was unable to stand.

The whisperer was gone! The Green Lama stepped to the doorway and looked into the hall. He could see no one.

He went back into the room, past the one man who was still conscious but lay there watching the Lama with fear in his eyes, and went to Evangl. He picked up one of the knives from the floor and cut her bonds. Then he did the same for Gary.

"THANK God you got here," Gary gasped, tearing the gag from his mouth. "You all right, darling?"

"Yes," Evangl said somewhat shakily. "J-just scared, that's all. How about you?"

"The same," Gary admitted. "We were trying to get to the shop to help you," he went on, turning to the Green Lama, "and this guy is out on the street and had a gun on us before I even know he's around."

"I know," the Green Lama said. "Magga saw you. She came to the rescue herself and was caught in turn. If she hadn't been able to get away, I wouldn't have known you were here. Just a minute and we'll get back to the ship."

He walked over to the native who was still conscious and bent over him.

"You have already learned," he said

in Spanish, "one thing which I can do with a touch of my fingers, but I can do much more. You will tell me who it was who was giving you orders?"

"I do not know, *Senor*," the man said.

The Green Lama made a gesture with his hand.

"No, *Senor!*" the man cried. He was so frightened he was drooling at the mouth. "I swear it! Upon the bones of my dead mother, I swear it. I do not know. We were told three months past to take orders from this one by our leader, the *Americano* from next door. Other than that I know nothing!"

"It is well that you speak the truth," the Green Lama said, deciding that the man was too frightened to lie. He reached out and pressed at the base of the skull. The native went limp.

"Come," the Green Lama said. Leaving the light burning down upon the two unconscious natives, they went out of the room, down the hallways and downstairs to the street. They could find no cab so they walked back to Cristobal.

"Wait a minute," the Green Lama said as they neared the ship. In a distance he saw the Military Police patrol. From his pocket he took a piece of paper and a pencil. He wrote: "You will find two more of the same gang unconscious in the house next to the shop. Good luck, soldiers." He then found a small stone, secured the paper to it and threw it towards the two soldiers. As he saw one of them go after the rock, he turned toward the ship. The sky above was already beginning to lighten.

"As you go up the gangplank," the Green Lama said to Gary, "ask the sailor on guard if anyone else recently came aboard. While you're doing that, I'll slip by him."

Gary and Evangl went ahead up the gangplank. The sleepy sailor greeted them with a limp salute and Gary asked his question. As the sailor considered his answer, a shadowy figure slipped up the gangplank unnoticed and went along the deck.

"Not right recent," the sailor said. "The last one to come aboard was the Spanish girl from Deck A. That must have been about an hour ago, sir. Is somebody missing?"

"I don't think so," Gary said.

"Well, if there is they better be getting here," the sailor said. "We'll be leaving here before long."

"I feel like sleeping all the way to Havana," Gary said. "Good night."

"Good night, sir," the sailor answered and went back to watching the sky turn luminous and pink in the east. Gary and Evangl went on to their staterooms.

CHAPTER IX

A Prisoner

 THE *S. S. Cathay* nosed into the heavy Atlantic waves, shook the water off and settled down for the next one. Two and a half days from Cristobal, ten hours out of Havana, she was running into her first bad weather. Dinner had been over some time, the stewards had tidied up and everything was quiet below. The few passengers who hadn't retired to their staterooms were either in the lounge or in the bar. A few were fortifying their courage with alcohol; others were watching them and gulping hastily at the thought of drinking anything.

Down on Deck C—deserted except for the patients in the hospital—the Green Lama was holding a council of war in the baggage room. The captain had discovered the morning that they left Cristobal that the Green Lama was missing and after a thorough search of the ship—during which time the Green Lama was hiding in the captain's own quarters—he had decided that their prisoner had escaped in Cristobal. He radioed the Army authorities at Cristobal and proceeded to put the whole unpleasant incident out of his mind.

First Mate Shallet and his friends in Suite A, however, were not quite so sure that the Green Lama had left them at the end of the Canal. They began to brighten up a little though when two days had passed without them receiving a visit.

Since the search, the Green Lama had spent his days sleeping in the baggage room and his nights roaming the ship looking for information. The quest had been fruitless.

This last night before reaching Havana, Gary, Dr. Valco and Ken Clayton were in the baggage room with the Green Lama. He had sent Gary after the other two.

"It's been more than a week since we left California," the Green Lama was saying, "and we still don't know who this unknown head of the smuggling ring is. I have narrowed the field down, but that is not enough. I believe that none of the gang knows whom they're taking orders from—unless it's Foran. He may know, since he's the one to report to the boss. Tomorrow another step in their smuggling is scheduled to take place in Havana. I know the plans so I can scotch that easily enough. But it still won't get us the leader."

"Why not get this Foran down here and ask him a few questions?" Ken Clayton asked. "If he does know maybe you can make him tell."

"That's an excellent idea," the Green Lama said, smiling in the darkness. "But the place for my questioning is in the cell downstairs. Gary, do you suppose you could deliver him down there, quietly and in one piece?"

James Nord

"Could I!" Gary said. "You want him?"

"I think we'll try it," the Green Lama said. "Get him if you can, without running any risk. Bring him to the cell in the hold. Doctor, if you and Ken want to string along, I suggest you follow me down instead of coming with me."

"We don't seem to be needed," grumbled Dr. Valco good-naturedly, "but I suppose we might as well go along and watch."

"Fine," the Green Lama said. He rose and went to the door. There was no one in the corridor and he let Gary out first. Then in a few minutes he left, taking the stairs that went into the hold. The doctor and Ken Clayton followed him shortly.

They had been waiting by the cell

for only fifteen or twenty minutes when there was the sound of steps coming down. Then Foran, walking very stiff but with a smile on his face, came into sight. Behind him came Gary, his right hand in his pocket.

"It was a cinch," Gary said. "He was at the bar and I just sidled up by him and let him get a feel of the .38 and he came along like a lamb."

"I don't know what you expect to gain by this," Foran said coldly, looking the bunch over.

"We thought," the Green Lama said equably, "that you might know who your leader is and would like to tell us. Do you know?"

"Maybe I do and maybe I don't. I overestimated you, Green Lama. Only a fool would pull a trick like this."

"PERHAPS," the Green Lama said. "There is an old proverb that has some bearing. I hope you don't mind my addiction to the old proverbs. But if a wise man, who can't swim, and a fool, who can, are both thrown into a pool of water, which then would you say is the wise man and which the fool?"

"I'm afraid I'm no good at riddles," Foran said. "But I still suggest the smartest thing you can do is let me go."

"We shall see," the Green Lama said. He stepped forward and, before Foran could guess what he was going to do, pressed both hands to the sides of Foran's head.* The latter's arms fell limply to his sides and a startled expression came over his face.

Then the Green Lama's right hand slid down and his fingers pressed lightly on Foran's throat.

"What the hell—" exclaimed Foran, but his voice was only a slight whisper.

* He had pressed on the precentral gyrus of rolando, the nerves which control the extremities. In this case, he had only paralyzed the arms.

By pressing on his throat, the Lama had partially paralyzed the vocal cords.

"I'll explain it to you," the Green Lama said softly. "You probably never heard of radioactive salts. But it's a way of charging the human body with electricity through the absorption of these radioactive salts into the blood stream. Very ingenious. With it, plus a knowledge of nerve centers, one can perform miracles. A sort of electrified *jiu jitsu*, only in this case a very slight pressure is all that's required.

"For example, Foran, I can by degrees paralyze every part of your body. I can also make you blind, deaf and speechless. Now, would you like to tell us what you know?"

"No," Foran said hoarsely. But for the first time the big, sandy-haired man looked uncertain. "You can't scare me with any of that phoney Oriental hocus-pocus."

"I don't want to frighten you," the Green Lama said. "I merely want to convince you. Like this." He reached out and touched the side of Foran's head. One of his legs suddenly buckled under him, throwing him to the floor. He managed to pull himself back up on the other leg and stood there defiantly with one leg hanging useless.

"Well?" the Green Lama said.

"Go to hell!" Foran whispered. The muscles in his face were drawing tighter and tighter.

"I'll leave you that one leg to stand on—for the time being," the Green Lama said. He reached out and pressed just in front of the man's ears.

"That paralyzed your face," the Green Lama said. "The effect of that isn't usually very startling so I don't suppose you have decided to talk. Have you?"

Foran only stared back with a mixture of hate and fear in his eyes. But slowly the fear was beginning to predominate. He was a man who could have stood almost any sort of third degree, but this slow crippling of all his muscles had too much of the eerie and his morale was breaking.

"It's terrible to be blind," the Green Lama said. "A hard enough pressure will blind you permanently, while a light touch will bring only temporary darkness. Like this." He reached up, touched the top of Foran's head. The man blinked as his vision was suddenly blotted out. He began trembling and his face was beaded with sweat.

"Shall I press harder, Foran?" the Green Lama asked softly.

For a moment there was silence, as the criminal struggled with himself. Then he broke. It was almost visible, as though you could see the man wilting inside.

"DAMN you to hell," he whispered. "I'll tell you, but you're killing me as sure as if you had your gunman pull the trigger."

"Who?" the Green Lama asked.

"I don't know," Foran said. "No! Don't touch me again! It's the truth. I don't know."

"Where do you report while on this ship?"

"The boss either comes to our suite or I get a code message put up on the bulletin board."

"I believe you," the Green Lama said. "Are there any more of the gang on this ship?"

"Not that I know of," Foran said.

"What are you picking up in Havana tomorrow? More dope?"

"No. Diamonds smuggled in from Holland."

"You'll smuggle them into New York in the things of Walters' that have already been examined, won't you?"

"Yes."

"That's the way you've worked it several times?"

"Yes," Foran whispered.

"What's the meaning of the death's head ring your leader wears?"

"He's the head of the murder syndicate in New York too. The one the D.A.'s cracking down on."

"Are you, Nord and Shallet in that too?"

"Shallet isn't. And I've never worked in that end. Nord is one of the executioners."

"Did you tell the truth about the distribution of dope to high school children the other night when you were talking to the gang in Colon?"

"Yes," Foran said, tonelessly.

"If you're not around tomorrow, who will pick up the diamonds in Havana?"

"Probably Shallet."

"Will the boss be there too?" the Green Lama asked.

"Probably. He usually is around somewhere when we do these jobs to see there's no upset."

"Where's the place?"

"On the western side of Havana, out of town. At Miguel Zamora's. He's the head of the Havana end."

"How many people will be there?" the Green Lama asked.

"Only Miguel himself when the diamonds are called for."

"Do you know who Mrs. Walters is, Foran?" the Green Lama asked.

"No."

"All right," the Green Lama said. "I'm going to put you in irons in one of these cells. The one, in fact, in which you helped place me. You will recover your eyesight in another thirty minutes. I expect you'll be found shortly, so you'll be fed, but I'm afraid you won't get out of the irons until we get to New York and I'm also afraid you won't be able to tell them anything."

As he finished speaking, the Green Lama reached over and struck a light blow on the vagus nerve branches, by the thyroid, paralyzing Foran's speech entirely.

"That will only last about a day," he said, "but I'll be back to renew it."

Using his little steel pick, the Green Lama unlocked the farthest cell and he and Gary half carried Foran in and set him down on the small bench. Again the pick came into use to unlock the leg irons and the handcuffs. They were fitted on Foran and locked. Then the Green Lama leaned over them with the sliver of steel again. After several minutes, he straightened up.

"It will take a blow-torch to get those off now," he said. He and Gary walked out and closed the cell door. The Green Lama locked it and again moved the pick around in the lock. Satisfied, he turned to the others.

"That clears up part of it," he said. "I think after tomorrow, I will know the answer to the rest of it. The boat docks in Havana at seven in the morning. The appointment with Zamora is for ten o'clock. So about nine-thirty, doctor, I want you to find some excuse to keep the captain in his quarters long enough for me to get off the boat as Dr. Pali. Gary, you and Evangl and Magga will keep watch to see who else leaves about the right time to make that appointment. I will follow Shallet. Ken—" he looked at the young actor for a minute—"you have shown a desire to help in the fight against evil and have earned the right to satisfy that desire— if you still have it. Would you like to come with me tomorrow?"

"You bet," Clayton said.

"All right. Watch by the gangplank tomorrow and when you see me leave, follow me. Now all of you go get some

rest for the morrow. *Tashi shog!*"

The three men filed up the stairs and several minutes later the shadowy figure of the Green Lama followed them.

CHAPTER X

Trapped!

EN CLAYTON stood by the gangplank of the ship, leaning against the railing, and watched the bustle on the dock below. Most of the shopping and sight-seeing passengers had already left the ship and the deck was pretty much deserted. A bunch of stevedores were rolling dice on the dock and this was what held his attention—ostensibly at least. Out of one corner of his eye, however, he kept a lookout for the Green Lama.

It was almost nine-thirty by his watch when he saw First Mate Shallet, in his shore whites, hurry along the deck and go down the gangplank. He seemed nervous, glancing over his shoulder every few minutes. Ken saw him climb into a cab.

The cab had no sooner pulled away than Ken saw the Green Lama, as Dr. Pali, stroll out on the deck and walk down the gangplank. Ken followed slowly.

The Green Lama stopped ahead and began to haggle with a cab driver. For a minute, Ken hesitated. But he couldn't just stand there, so he walked on slowly. Then as he almost reached the Green Lama, the latter seemed to strike a bargain and jumped into the cab. As the driver climbed in the front, the Green Lama leaned out and motioned to Ken. He stepped into the cab beside the Lama and they were off.

"You know the Zamora house?" the Green Lama asked the cab driver.

"Like I know my mother-in-law, *Senor*," the driver said sourly, "which is to say, too well. The *Senor* could choose a better place to go."

"Not for my purpose," the Green Lama said, smiling at Ken.

"The *Senor* knows best," the driver said, shrugging. He stepped on the gas and whirled the car around a couple of tourists.

Within a few minutes they were out of the main part of Havana and whipping along a smooth highway, lined on each side with such a riotous blaze of tropical flowers as to be almost blinding. Scattered along here were beautiful mansions, set back from the road amidst palm trees.

"There is the Zamora house just ahead, *Senor*," the driver said, slowing down and pointing to a huge white mansion a few hundred yards ahead.

"Good. Stop here," the Green Lama ordered. The cab jerked to a stop.

The Green Lama and Ken Clayton got out and the Lama paid the driver, who turned his cab around and drove back toward Havana, shaking his head.

"Come," the Green Lama said. He led the way into the field on the right. Ahead of them was a grove of palm trees, going up almost to the side of the house that was their objective. They cut through the field and were soon in the grove. When they reached the other side, there was an open space of not more than twenty feet before the house. They were on the side, next to what was obviously the servant's entrance. Around to the front, they could see the rear end of the cab that had brought Shallet.

"If only Zamora and Shallet are there," the Green Lama said, "they are probably in the study which should not be on the same side as the servant's entrance, if I've guessed right. However,

we'll have to risk it. Want to wait here for me?"

"Not a chance," Ken said.

Taking another look at the blank windows facing them, the Green Lama left the grove and sauntered slowly to-

Evangl Stewart

ward the house, Ken Clayton following immediately behind him. From a distance, it would have appeared merely that a rather handsome priest and a young man were coming to the house, possibly for a drink of water after a long hike through the fields. That was partly what the Green Lama was gambling on should someone catch a glimpse of them.

Reaching the servant's entrance, the Green Lama tried the door. It was locked. He reached in his pocket and brought out the steel pick. In a minute the door swung open. The two men stepped into a dark corridor.

They halted just inside the door and listened, but there was not a sound in the house. Nodding to Ken to follow, the Green Lama slipped silently along the hall toward the front of the house.

THEN somewhere ahead of them they heard the closing of a door and the sudden roar of the taxi motor in front of the house. The two men rounded a turn in the hall and came into a corridor that led to the front door. On both sides rooms opened off. The Green Lama stopped and listened. The only sound he could hear was the slight breathing of Ken Clayton behind him. There was something unnatural in the silence and the Green Lama felt uneasy. Then he heard a slight sound to one side. He looked around quickly.

A door had opened, almost noiselessly, and a tall good-looking man, with a tiny waxed mustache, stood in the doorway. In his hands was a sub-machine gun, pointing directly at the Green Lama. The man was smiling.

"Pardon me, *Senors*," he said, "for not meeting you at the door despite the fact that I was expecting you." He spoke with only a faint trace of accent. "I believe you were looking for me, Don Miguel Beigbeder y Atienzo Zamora. I am at your service. Will you come in?" He gestured with the machine gun and the Green Lama and Ken Clayton walked toward him. He walked backwards into the room.

"Not too fast, *Senor*," he said, looking at the Green Lama. "I have already heard of your speed and your ability to overcome difficulties. So do not rush the little machine gun." He smiled, showing a flash of white teeth.

As the Green Lama advanced into the room, he caught a glimpse of another figure, seated in an easy chair. Despite the warm weather, this figure wore a light-weight topcoat and a silk muffler was thrown across the face. Only the eyes, beneath the hatbrim, showed, and they were filled with cruel amusement. On the third finger of the right hand there was a silver and jade ring.

"Greetings, Green Lama," the figure said, speaking in a whisper. "Was this not a clever trap?"

"You knew I would be here?" the Green Lama asked calmly.

"Yes. I knew that you had not vanished in Colon as the stupid captain thought. I also knew that you would eavesdrop on the conversations of my men. So I had them talk about the meeting with Senor Zamora, the time and the place. Then you captured Foran—" for a moment the eyes filled with hate—"and probably got a verification from him. That insured your coming. They did not know it was a trap. Only *Senor* Zamora and I knew that.

"You have been troublesome to me, Green Lama. So far you have done no great damage, but you might. Then, too, there is another inducement. You probably know of my affiliation with another organization in New York—" the death's head ring was brought into obvious view—"which at present is in some difficulty. Last night I received a cablegram in response to one about you and learned that certain other interests there will pay us fifty thousand dollars for proof that you are dead. That is a good price and will make up for the fact that we will have to kill your friends without compensation. It was nice of you to bring one of them along. We will get the others later."

"The wolf always worries when the hunter draws near," the Green Lama said. He was watching Zamora for the slightest opening, but there was none. "I have almost all the answers."

"All but the one you wanted to know most—my identity," the whisperer said, laughing hoarsely.

"That I will know soon," the Green Lama said quietly. For the first time since entering the room he was hopeful. Across the room, he had noticed another door opening slowly. It might be help—or it might not.

"I'm afraid not," the voice said. "This time there will be no mistake of locking you up. Miguel will kill you immediately. There is no house close and the shots will not be noticed. One of his men is at the rear of the house and will dispose of your bodies. Now, Miguel, fire!"

The Cuban's face tightened with resolve and he steadied the machine gun.

From where the Green Lama had seen the door opening, there was a whiplike crack of a small gun. Blood spurted from the Cuban's right hand and the machine gun dropped to the floor. He began cursing in Spanish as he gripped his hand.

Through the door came the redhead from the ship, Jean Farrell. She was holding a small automatic, smoke trickling from the barrel, in her right hand.

"JUST relax—" she began, only to break off and fire again. Splinters flew from the door back of the Green Lama—but the muffled figure was gone. While the Green Lama and Ken had been gazing at the girl, the leader had jumped for the door. The Green Lama, expecting Gary or Magga but certainly not this girl, had been so startled that for a brief second, he had forgotten about the other occupant of the room.

Now he leaped out of the door into the hallway in pursuit. The outer door was just closing. He raced to it and jerked it open. As he did there was the roar of a motor and a small car, bearing Havana license plates, lurched forward and tore through the gate. The Green Lama shrugged and returned to the room.

Miguel Zamora still stood in the center of the room, clutching his hand and cursing. Ken had jumped forward and now held the machine gun, although he was looking at the redhead.

"What are you doing here?" the Green Lama asked her as he came back in.

"I might ask the same thing," she said flippantly. "But to tell the truth I wanted to know what was going on. This ham actor here failed to follow me around this morning for the first time. So I smelled a mystery right away. When I saw you both go off, I followed. I also followed through the fields and woods—and tore a damn good pair of silk hose doing it, too. When I got to the back of the house,

some weasel tried to stop me. I don't mind a guy taking a pass at me but when he does it with a gun, it's too much. So I put one on his head and came on in.

"Machine guns always make me nervous so when I saw that guy pointing one, I stopped him. But that last shot was lousy," she ended ruefully.

"As long as the first one wasn't," the Green Lama said. "We'll get the other person yet. Do you always carry a gun, Miss Farrell?"

"Call me Jean or I'll feel like an old maid school teacher," the redhead grinned. "I've been carrying this gun ever since I can remember. My dad was an old-time westerner and he always claimed that a girl wasn't decently dressed unless she wore long woollen underwear and carried a gun. Hell, I got to do at least one thing he wanted me to."

"What a girl!" Ken Clayton said, softly.

"I'm inclined to agree with you," the Green Lama said, smiling. "Especially since she saved our lives after my carelessness put us in this trap."

"Men always get careless if there isn't a woman around to look after them," Jean said.

The Green Lama smiled and went over to Zamora. He took a handkerchief from his pocket, tore it into strips and dressed the wounded hand. Then he struck a quick blow at the base of Zamora's skull. The Cuban crumpled to the floor.

"That ought to be good for people suffering from insomnia," Jean said as she saw the result of the blow. "How long will that last?"

"A couple of hours," the Green Lama said. He went out of the room toward the back. A minute later he appeared dragging the man Jean had knocked out

with her gun. Although this one was already unconscious, the Lama also tapped him at the base of the skull. Then he hurriedly went through a large desk that stood in the corner, nodding when he found a small book filled with dates and figures. He left it on the desk.

"Come on," he said. "There's still another car outside. We'll borrow it since I doubt if Senor Zamora will have any more use for it. We've just about enough time to make it back to the boat safely."

"You going to leave these two glamor boys here?" Jean asked, nodding at the two Cubans on the floor.

"Yes," the Green Lama said. "We'll get word to the police later to pick them up." The three of them went out and climbed into the other car sitting in the driveway.

Leaving Ken and Jean at the dock, after telling Ken to find Gary and send him down to the baggage room, the Green Lama managed to get back aboard without being noticed. He slipped down the back stairs to Deck C and into the baggage room unnoticed.

A little later there was a slight tapping on the door and he opened the door and let Gary in. Quickly, he outlined the events of the past hour to Gary.

"Who left the ship about the right time to get there before we did?" he asked when he had finished.

"The only one to leave," Gary said, "was that Mrs. Forbes. She left shortly before Shallet did and then came back just a little while ago. She was carrying some kind of bag."

"She was also one of those who received a number of cablegrams from New York," the Green Lama said.

"You think she's the head of the smuggling ring?" Gary asked. "Why she seems like just another talkative dame to me."

"She might be," the Green Lama said. "We'll see. In the meantime, I want you to send a cablegram to the Havana police, telling them to go out and pick up Zamora. Tell them the proof of his smuggling activities is in a little book on his desk.

"Then send another cablegram to Lieutenant Caraway* in New York and ask him to meet this boat when it docks in New York in three days."

CHAPTER XI

The Man With The Death's Head Face

IT WAS late afternoon when the *S. S. Cathay* moved slowly up North River and docked at the foot of West 21st Street in New York. The setting sun glinted dully from the rearing spire of the Empire State Building in the distance and, to the passengers waiting to get off, it seemed as though the tugs guiding the steamer were practically standing still. It wasn't until Gary brought word that the ship had already tied up at the pier that the Green Lama left the baggage room and made his way up the passageway and out onto the deck.

At one end of the deck Captain Betts was surrounded by cops. He too had radioed ahead for the police to board the ship at the dock and this was the reason none of the passengers had been allowed to disembark. Now he was telling his story to the officers. To one side was the tall, lean figure of Lieutenant John Caraway, whose eyes ranged the deck as he listened.

"There he is!" Captain Betts suddenly shouted, as he saw the Green Lama

---

*He was referring to Lieutenant John Caraway, head of a Special Crime Squad in New York City. Caraway was the man who helped the Green Lama, and received the credit, in the case of *The Crimson Hand* and the *Crooms of Murder*.

---

come up. "That man dressed as a priest and calling himself Father Pali. Some kind of heathen. He's the one that is the head of the smuggling ring and who killed the men on board my ship!"

The police, headed by a red-faced

Gary Brown

V.E.P

Sergeant, surged toward the Green Lama. Lieutenant Caraway stepped forward, a smile on his somewhat cynical face. He was one of the few people in New York who knew that Dr. Pali and the Green Lama were one.

"Just a minute, Sergeant," he said. "I know this man that the captain is accusing. In fact, he sent me a cablegram asking me to meet the ship."

The sergeant hesitated. He knew Caraway's reputation as an honest cop; that the commissioner, because of it, had appointed him the head of the Special Crime Squad.

"Okay, Lieutenant," he said, saluting.

"Hello, Father Pali," Lieutenant Caraway said, turning to the Green Lama and holding out his hand.

"Hello, Lieutenant," the Green Lama said, shaking hands with Caraway.

"What's all this mess about?" Caraway asked. "You know?"

"Most of it," the Green Lama answered. "That, plus the fact that the captain thinks I'm guilty of murder, was why I wired you. I've spent most of the past week down in the baggage room just so the captain couldn't keep me chained up."

"Captain!" a woman demanded, pushing up through the row of policemen. "I demand that you let me off the boat this minute. My husband is down there on the dock waiting for me and I refuse to be treated like a criminal."

The Green Lama looked at the woman and smiled. "That was really very kind of you to come over here, Mrs. Forbes," he said. "We were just going to look for you."

The woman looked up at him. "Oh, Dr. Pali! I didn't see you. Doctor, can't you do something about making the captain let me off this boat?"

"Yes, I can, Mrs. Forbes," he said. He turned to Caraway. "This is one of your arrests, Lieutenant," he said. "She appears quite harmless but she is the head of the smuggling ring and is also connected with the murder ring you're cleaning up over in Brooklyn."

"Why! I never—" gasped Mrs. Forbes.

"Are you sure?" Caraway asked tensely.

"Positive," the Green Lama said.

"GRAB her," Caraway said to the cops. Two of the burly patrolmen reached for Mrs. Forbes arms. As they did, her face changed from one of querulous anger to hatred and her right hand fumbled with the bag she was carrying. The cops stepped in quickly and there was a short tussle.

Then the cops had her by both arms and one of them was holding the small automatic she had been trying to take from her purse.

"Now," the Green Lama said, "if you'll look in her purse, I think you'll also find a small ring with a jade death's head surrounded by a silver inverted pentagram. Unless I'm mistaken that has something to do with the murder ring here in New York."

Lieutenant Caraway nodded. "We found rings like that on several of the top men in the ring," he said. One of the cops had already gone into the purse and he handed the ring to Caraway.

"Now what's the rest of the story, Father?" Caraway asked the Green Lama.

"This part of it is smuggling." the Green Lama said. "You'll find all the loot somewhere among the things down in the cabin that was taken under the name of Walters. They picked up a load of diamonds in Havana, but that was only a sideline. And, incidentally, the Havana police have the man at that end.

"The real line was dope; cocaine and opium, but mostly the former. The opium, I believe, was brought on from somewhere in California. You can check that later. The cocaine was picked up in Colon, in the Panama Canal Zone. I think all of the men there are now in the hands of either the Colon police or the Army authorities in Cristobal.

"They had a plan to sell the cocaine to high school children throughout the United States—quite a clever plan I might say. Their peddlers were to go around ostensibly selling comic magazines. The innocent buyers *would* get an ordinary comic magazine for the regular price, but the knowing ones would get a magazine that had an envelope of cocaine inserted in it. I imagine they were going to use the usual method of getting the kids addicted; have one man go around and throw parties at which the kids would be given cocaine without knowing it."

"Any more in the gang?" Caraway asked tersely.

"Yes," the Green Lama said. "Originally there were four others, but now there are three. One of them, Captain Betts will be interested to know, is First Mate Shallet of this boat. I suspected you'll find him down in his quarters."

Lieutenant Caraway nodded to a couple of plainclothesmen and they slipped away.

"The other two men are Terrill Foran and James Nord who had Suite A on Deck B. I took the precaution of capturing Nord last night. Foran has been a prisoner down in the hold since Havana, although I believe that Shallet and Nord kept it quiet. And I'm afraid you'll need a blowtorch to get him out of the leg-irons and handcuffs. You'll find Nord down there in the cell next to the one Foran's in."

At Caraway's nod a couple more cops went toward the stairway leading below.

"They connected with the murder ring?" Caraway asked.

"NORD and Foran are, although I don't think Shallet is," the Green Lama answered. "Foran and Shallet, incidentally, are the men who murdered the other member of the gang, Carlos Lopez, just after he had killed Captain Betts' Second Mate. They did it under the impression that they were killing me. Fortunately, they were mistaken."

"How'd you get wise to her?" Caraway asked, nodding towards Mrs. Forbes.

"She was on my list from the beginning although I was disinclined to think of a woman as the leader. Then, too, the leader dressed as a man, and the whisper she used disguised her voice. But she was one of the suspects who had been sending and receiving many cablegrams. When I reflected further about that whisper, there seemed to be little reason for it unless there was something about the voice that *had* to be masked. A woman would have a reason. Then in Colon when the leader ordered the men to cut and mar a girl's face, it struck me more as the psychological action of a vindictive, jealous woman than of a man. Final proof, however, came in Havana when she was the only one who left the boat, and returned, to coincide with the movements of the leader. And that, I guess, Lieutenant Caraway, winds up the whole thing."

"Not quite," Captain Betts broke in. "How about that man Walters who went overboard the first night out?"

"Oh yes, Mr. Walters," the Green Lama said, smiling. "You see, there really wasn't any Mr. Walters. I kept thinking the answer to the whole thing in some way centered around him.

"Some member of the gang came on board the ship as Mr. Walters in San Francisco. He was evidently careful to be inconspicuous, so that no one would be able to give a good description of him later. He set the stage in the cabin and walked off at Los Angeles. Then Foran just waited until he was alone on deck and yelled 'Man overboard.'

"Incidentally, I kept thinking there was something familiar about Mrs. Forbes. When finally I was certain she was the leader, it occurred to me that she somewhat resembled the photograph of Mrs. Walters in the cabin. She evidently went home as soon as the boat landed, changed her appearance and came back to collect the things of her dearly departed husband.

"Those things had all been examined thoroughly. So they were handed over to her. The smuggled goods had been added, in the meantime, after the boat left Havana. By the virtue of non-existence, Mr. Walters was very handy."

"Sort of the man who wasn't there, huh?" one of the cops said.

"You might say that," the Green Lama said, "although in Tibet we would say that man who cannot be seen is perhaps non-existent rather than invisible."

Two of the plainclothesmen arrived at this point with Shallet manacled between them.

"Well," Caraway said, turning to the captain, "I guess you can let your passengers disembark now, Captain Betts. We seem to have our prisoners."

Captain Betts turned and gave orders to the sailors standing by the gangplank.

"A swell job," Caraway said, turning back to the Green Lama. "I—" He broke off as he saw there was no one standing next to him. The Green Lama had vanished.

A LITTLE later, as the Green Lama went across the dock toward the street and a cab, he found four people waiting for him. They were Gary, Evangl, Ken Clayton and Jean Farrell.

"Dr. Valco said to tell you he hoped to see you soon," Gary said. "He wanted to get to his office, so he hurried off."

"And Magga?" the Lama asked.

"We haven't seen her since the boat docked," Gary said.

"Look—*Tulku*," Evangl said, "Gary and I have decided we're going to get married whether my mother likes it or not, and we wondered if you'd marry us?"

The Green Lama smiled. "Your mother may accept Gary as a son-in-law," he said, "but I doubt if she would ever accept a marriage performed by a Buddhist priest. But I'll come to the wedding if you'll let me know."

"You bet we will," Gary said. "And —look chief—maybe I'm getting married, but I just wanted you to know that I'm still going to be around to help you when you need me."

"That's all right," the Green Lama said. "We'll see. It is written that the man who marries is already in debt to safety. But may Buddha bless you both. *Om! Ma-ni pad-me Hum!*"

"So long, chief," Gary said, shaking hands.

"Goodby, *Tulku*," Evangl said softly. She turned her face up and kissed the Green Lama lightly on the cheek.

"Er—look," Ken Clayton said as the Lama was about to turn away. "I just wanted to tell you that I'm going to be in New York from now on and if you need any help, I'd like you to count me in. I'm going to be staying at the Welton Hotel. I mean—that is if you think I can be of any help . . ."

The Green Lama smiled again. "There is always room at the feet of justice," he said. "I will remember."

"Hey, wait a minute," Jean Farrell said. "If Beautiful here thinks he's going to hang on my bustle around Broadway all the time and then leave me at the church door when the fun starts, he's got another think on the way up. If he's going to make a pass at Justice, at least I ought to get to sit on the sidelines. What's she got that I haven't! Of course, maybe I get a little scared at the sight of a machine gun . . ."

"I can use that fear," the Green Lama said with a chuckle. "I'll remember you both. Now, good night." He turned and left them. At the street, he got into a cab and directed it to an address on Park Ave.

Still dressed as Dr. Pali, the Green Lama entered the private entrance of the Park Avenue building and rode in the elevator up to the penthouse that was his headquarters. He walked swiftly through the dark rooms to the laboratory in the rear.

After a while he went to a workbench on the other side of the room and switched on a small radio hidden in the panels of the bench. The voice of a news commentator came in through the loudspeaker.

". . . shot down two Nazi planes over the channel today . . . Flash! According to a bulletin just received, James "Death's Head" Nord, suspected gunman for the murder ring, tonight killed a policeman and escaped while officers were taking him to headquarters from a boat where he had been arrested. The slain officer was Patrolman Fred Lawton. Lieutenant John Caraway has asked everyone to be on the lookout for the escaped killer. He is about six feet tall, sunken eyes, prominent cheek bones—"

The Green Lama switched off the radio and stood staring into space. The room was silent except for the clicking of the prayer wheel.

"I will also remember," the Green Lama said softly, "the Man With The Death's Head Face. It is written that the man of violence must some day face the wrath of the gods . . ."

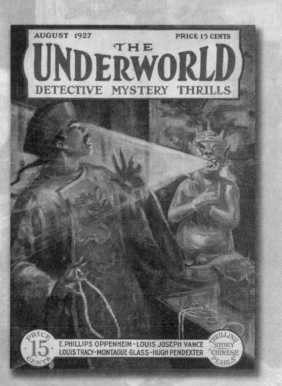

The TWISTED MEN

A Complete Novelette of Eerie Thrills
By HUGH B. CAVE
Author of "The Preying Hands," "Rendezvous," etc.

CHAPTER I

Mad Laughter

I COULD make this story very personal, but I'm not going to. That would be the easiest way, but when I got through you'd be apt to look me up—just for the satisfaction of calling me some kind of liar. So we'll call the fellow Peter Smith and name his wife Jo, which will make it easier and perhaps keep it on the rational side of that thin fence between sanity and madness.

If Peter Smith had been driving his car alone on the Mendon Road that night when the gods of disaster

---

The Virus of Idiocy was in that Vile Potion

The eyes of the woman glittered in shadow-pits of madness

screamed their opening chorus, he probably would have kept right on going. But he happened to be with Jo, and he'd been married to Jo, then, for just three weeks. And when that wail of terror ripped through the rain, Jo put a trembling hand on her husband's arm and gasped out, thickly: "Peter! What was that?"

So Peter braked the car to a stop.

Clutched in a Dead Man's Hand

It was a lonely road, a winding black trail of patched macadam in the heavily wooded mountain region of northern New England. Midnight had gone half an hour ago. Since the slumbering town of Courtney had slipped past, some eight miles back, the machine's headlights hadn't picked out a single sign of human habitation.

Now there was a light winking in the murk, through a fringe of wind-bent trees, and the light was screaming.

At least, something or someone in the rambling farmhouse there was screaming, and the voice was bellowing like a mad thing through the rain and the dark. And Jo was saying again, in a frightened whisper: "Peter, what *is* it? Someone is in trouble!"

Peter Smith looked into his wife's face and saw that she was scared. He himself had no yen to go ploughing out into the rain, or to investigate queer things that didn't concern him in the least.

But something about that ghastly voice in the night *was* terrifying. Something abnormal hung in it. The voice seemed to be laughing and shrieking at the same time, and the laughter was blood-curdling.

"You sit tight," Peter said. "I'll go see what's wrong."

He got out of the car and slopped through the dark. The shrieking had stopped then. It began again while he was striding up the boardwalk to the veranda. When he got that far, he stopped and looked behind him, wondering if he were doing an unwise thing in leaving Jo alone in the car. If something really were wrong here. . . .

But the yammering voice lured him forward. He thumped on the veranda steps and knocked on the half-open door. The sound of his big knuckles against wet door-panels was gulped by a peal of unholy laughter which came yowling from the house. Laughter? Peter wasn't sure of that. Whatever the ghastly sound was, it had passed beyond the bounds of sanity.

And a woman was making it.

Peter Smith sucked damp air into his big chest and went over the threshold, went slowly down the narrow corridor that yellowed away before him. He got to an open doorway and stopped there, and stared into an old-fashioned living-room.

His legs hardened under him. His mouth jerked open and his teeth dug into his twisted lower lip. He said aloud, "My God!"—but the words were lost in a new crescendo of mad laughter from the gargoyle face of the woman who sat there before him.

SHE was a young woman, not as young as Jo, perhaps, but not over thirty either. That is, her body was young. Her face was something out of a wax museum, pale and dirty and horrible, with a gluey mass of black hair twisting down one side of it.

She had enormous eyes that looked at Peter Smith and bored through him, and her discolored lips were curled out of shape from screaming. But she wasn't screaming now. She was laughing. There are many kinds of laughter.

The woman sat on an old hair sofa with her arms wrapped around her knees and her head lolling grotesquely with every lurching movement of her shoulders. She sat and laughed. The room was full of the wail of her voice, and Peter Smith cringed from the din. Then he heard something else—a door opening to one side. He jerked around and uttered a guttural scream of his own. Of horror.

The door creaked back against withered wall-paper, and over the threshold twisted a thing that looked like a crippled dog. Peter's brain registered the word "dog" before jerking to the truth. The crawling thing was human.

The woman stared at it and went off on another frightful splurge of insane mirth. The man wriggled into the room and stopped, and looked at Peter.

Peter wanted suddenly to shriek and run. His numbed legs wouldn't let him.

The woman stopped laughing and

screamed luridly: "Look at him! Take a good look at him, mister! That's Bert Crandall—that's my husband—that's the man I married—look at him! I told him not to go out of this house tonight! I warned him. Now look at him! He's twisted like the others!"

The woman was mad. Any woman would have gone mad, seeing her husband like that. Peter Smith, who was a stranger and had no personal interest in the man, felt things cracking in his own brain and had to hang onto himself, had to smother his terror under the frantic thought that this thing was not real. It couldn't be real!

The man on the floor was twisted horribly, his back humped, his head curled under one lumpy shoulder. He crawled sluggishly on one knee, one ankle, the flat of his hands. His eyes were lumps of pale glass gaping piteously at the mad woman who was his wife. His face was the sagging putty-mask of an idiot. No coordination of muscles. No control.

Maybe he'd been good-looking once. Maybe he'd been straight and strong and normal. Not now.

"Someone ought to kill him," Peter kept thinking.

The house was cold, damp, and Peter shuddered. The twisted man had stopped crawling; he swayed there with the upper half of his body propped on stiff arms, his head lurching, a wet lump of tongue slobbering in his mouth. He made animal sounds, and then there was another sound out in the corridor. Jo—calling Peter's name.

Peter didn't want her to see. Once you saw that frightful thing you might never forget it. He jerked around, pawing the side of the doorframe.

But Jo was already beside him, staring.

The mad woman was staring, too. She pushed herself off the sofa and twisted forward, glaring. Glaring savagely, as if blaming Jo for what had happened to the pitiful creature on the floor. Jo stood transfixed.

The woman pushed Peter aside and put a clawing hand on Jo's arm. Her eyes glittered in sunken shadow-pits of madness. "Who are you? What'd you come here for?" she snarled.

Jo, pale and afraid, stood there rigid, with one arm caught in the fierce grip of the woman's fingers. Those fingers were powerful; they dug deep into Jo's smooth skin and made white blotches. But Jo couldn't answer. Her lips twitched, tried to make words, but no words were audible.

"Klinger sent you!" the mad woman shrieked. "Klinger sent you here to spy on me, to see what his filthy curse did to my man! I'll kill you, same as I'll kill him if I ever get my hands on him! Sure as my name's Nora Crandall—"

SHE hurled herself at Jo and stabbed both hands up to get hold of Jo's gaping eyes. Peter Smith intervened just in time. The mad woman would have torn the tongue out of Jo's screaming mouth.

Peter's flailing arm caught the woman across the throat and slammed her in a shrieking heap to the floor. "Run!" he bellowed at Jo. "For God's sake get out of here!"

He pushed her and stood swaying on wide-spread legs in the doorway, facing Nora Crandall. The mad woman scrambled to her feet, snarled toward him and jerked back again, retching, when the flat of his hand caught her across the face.

She didn't charge again. She stood gasping, her chest heaving enormously under the drenched cotton of her dress. Her eyes narrowed and drank in a long look at Peter's face, cataloging that face for the future.

"I'll kill you," she gritted. "I'll kill both of you—and Klinger, too, even if it takes me years. You turned my man into one of the twisted ones, and you'll pay for it!"

She didn't scream those words. They were uttered with a cold-blooded deliberation that burned its way into Peter's soul and seared his brain. He backed away slowly. Jo was calling to him, pleading with him to hurry. He pushed the door shut and went staggering down the hall toward her.

A peal of mad laughter pursued him into the night.

When he got into the car his face was drenched with sweat and his hands were slimy on the wheel. Jo, huddled beside him, was sobbing wretchedly.

CHAPTER II
A Message

THE village of Greendon was Jo's birthplace. Born here, she had lived with an old maid aunt after the death of her parents. Had attended Greendon's rural schools, gone to Durham to college, gone from there to Boston to become secretary to a Beacon Street physician. Met Peter and married him.

"Some day, Peter, if you go for the idea, we'll buy a summer home back in Greendon."

"Think so, sweet?"

"You'll love it there!"

Her desires were Peter's Bible. "Sure thing, Jo. We'll do it."

Jo had written letters—one to her aunt, another to Josiah Deemer who owned and ran the Greendon Inn, another to young Russell Polk, Greendon lawyer. A reply from Polk was in her chamois handbag now. Could she come to Greendon right away? If so, there might be a possibility of buying the Klinger estate at a ludicrously low price. Mr. Klinger had expressed a desire to sell. . . .

Peter remembered the letter as he braked the machine in front of the Greendon Inn. *Klinger* had expressed a desire to sell! And in that house of the twisted thing two miles behind them, a mad woman had shrieked: "Klinger sent you here to see what his filthy curse did to my man!"

He helped his wife out of the car and dragged luggage out after her. The hour was late now; one-thirty at least. Back in Portland Jo had said: "We'll get to Greendon too late to go to Aunt Mary's. But Mr. Deemer will have room for us at the inn."

Deemer, he thought, would probably be in bed. He slung a bag under each arm and climbed the steps slowly. You couldn't see much in the dark, but the inn had a long veranda, had half a dozen crazy roof-angles from which rain-water dribbled in a hollow dirge.

Jo pulled the agate bell-knob, put a hand on Peter's arm. "That woman, Peter. If I live to be a hundred, I'll never forget." As if in answer, the jingle of the old-fashioned bell came like mocking laughter from within the building. Peter was silent, thinking of the name Klinger.

"He's a recluse, sort of," Jo had said. "A retired professor. Lives alone in that lovely house."

The door creaked, swung open. Peter peered into a weak-lipped face under whitish hair. A pleasant enough face, twisted now into a frown which indicated bewilderment at the arrival of guests at such an hour.

DEEMER blinked near-sighted eyes. "Well, for heaven's sake, it's Miss Jo!"

"Mrs. Peter Smith now, Josiah. This is my husband."

Deemer stuck out a bony hand and hung onto Peter's big fist. He grinned, kept on grinning while Jo and Peter followed him inside, into a kitchen where a lamp glowed warmly on a table cluttered with newspapers. A thin, parchment-faced man stood up jerkily and did some staring.

"I reckon you remember Tom Unwin, the postmaster," Deemer said.

"Why, of course I do!"

"Funny thing, we were just talkin' about you, Jo. Lawyer Polk was tellin' us you were aimin' to buy up some property. He acted mighty pleased to think you'd be comin' back, and I reckon that's natural enough, ain't it, him havin' been so sweet on you all these years? Uh-huh!"

Peter stiffened a little. Jo flushed. Tom Unwin said, "I'll be gettin' on home, I reckon," and walked to the door—a small, stiff man, perhaps fifty years of age.

Peter took a long look at Josiah Deemer and felt uneasy. There was something about Deemer. Something queer, distasteful. His long white hair, perhaps, or the continuous twitching of his bony hands. Those hands kept pawing at Jo's arms as if seeking to clutch warm flesh.

Jo was saying: "There's a house up the road about two miles, Josiah. A small farmhouse, set back behind some trees. The woman's name is Nora. Nora Crandall." She shuddered, as if hearing that name again from the shrieking lips of the woman herself. "Do you know those people?"

He blinked his near-sighted eyes. "Nora and Bert Crandall? Sure! Bert was over here tonight, talkin' to Lawyer Polk about buyin' the Klinger place."

Jo didn't get that. It didn't register. "Something terrible—at that house," she said queerly. "A doctor should be sent there."

"Huh? What for?"

"I'll tell you what for!" Peter said grimly. "Nora Crandall is insane and her husband is ill. He's"—he used the mad woman's words without realizing it—"one of the twisted men, if that means anything to you!"

It meant much. Josiah Deemer stiffened convulsively and put a trembling hand out to clutch at the table. A slow, creeping wave of terror undulated through him, forcing his eyes from their sockets. "One of the twisted men!" he croaked. "Oh, my God, no! Not Bert Crandall! Not another!"

"Easy now. Easy." Peter put an arm around him and helped him to a chair. Jo went to the big iron sink and brought water, and made Deemer drink. The man sat with his head forward, long arms dangling. He was breathing dangerously hard for one no longer young.

"Klinger's doin' it. He said he'd do it, when they ran him out of town. Said he'd be back—"

"What is this about Klinger?" Jo demanded.

"It's him turnin' Greendon into a village of death. Crandall's the third

—the third of the twisted men—"

"What are you talking about?"

He jerked his head up and blinked into Jo's stare. "It begun when they ran Endren Klinger out of town," he mumbled. "Some of the women folk was complainin' about him sneakin' out of his house late o' nights and prowlin' around the village, starin' at people and scarin' 'em. They claimed he was part crazy. So the men folk ordered him to leave—and he left—swearing he'd return to get even.

"Three weeks to a month ago, that was. Last week Cap'n Whaley died, all twisted and broken an'—an' mad. Doctor Glending done all that was possible, but it wasn't no kind of disease Glending ever seen before. Then Moley Anderson was took, and he left a wife and two grown-up daughters, and they near went crazy along with him. Now Bert Crandall—" Deemer pushed the heel of one hand against his eyes and rubbed tears out of them. "I better go for Doctor Glending. Maybe this time he'll be able to do somethin'. You two can take a room upstairs."

Peter and Jo stared hard while the old man hunched himself erect and scuffed to the door. Jo said: "We'll go upstairs, Peter." Her voice was low; her hand on Peter's arm was cold as a lump of ice.

He scooped up the luggage and trailed her along a musty corridor, up a flight of uncarpeted stairs that creaked under his weight. His first impression of this house had been correct; the building was a farmhouse made over, huge and rambling, built to no standard pattern. "Gloomy joint," he muttered.

"Yes, it is," Jo said, "but—"

She stopped with a jerk. A shut door loomed in shadows beside her, and from beyond it came a voice, a shrill voice, thin as a child's. "Josiah! You, Josiah! Is that you?"

Peter scowled in bewilderment as the door opened, spilling yellow light into the hall. He stared at the young fellow who stood there. Stared at a thin sallow face, a mop of untrimmed hair above eyes none too intelligent.

The spectral death-mask studied him

"Oh," the fellow said. "I thought you was Josiah."

Jo smiled. "You remember me, Dommy? I'm Josephine Lawlor. Remember?"

The young fellow gaped, astonished. "Jo! Why, Jo Lawlor!"

Jo introduced Peter. "This is Dommy Laughton, Peter. He and I grew up together in this town." And Peter nodded, frowning.

Later Peter said: "Dommy Laughton, eh? Who is he?"

"He's Josiah's orphaned nephew." Jo had reached the end of the hall, opened a door, now, and stood on the threshold, sniffing. "This is one of Josiah's best rooms. It's kind of musty, but with the windows opened . . ."

Peter closed the door behind him.

It was a small room, but it had a couple of chairs and a bed, and would do for the night. Tomorrow night they'd be at the home of Jo's Aunt Mary. Peter was glad of that.

While Jo was undressing he went to a window and stared out into drooling darkness. There wasn't much you could like about Jo's home town on a night like this. Well, he needed sleep. Maybe in the morning—

Outside, someone was screaming.

It came like that, came suddenly, without warning, grinding into Peter's morbid thoughts and jerking him back as he started sluggishly away from the window. Someone was screaming. The sound belched up from the street in front of the inn and knifed through rain and darkness and pulled Peter's eyes forward in their sockets.

Jo cried thickly: "What is it, Peter?" Jo was naked except for the bottom half of a pair of pajamas, and she ran around the bed in her bare feet and pounded to the window. Peter put an arm around her.

It was dark down there and something was moving. Something was running toward the hotel, screaming and shouting incoherently. Jo said: "It's Josiah!"

"You stay here," Peter growled. "Get some clothes on!" Then he went ploughing to the door.

He raced past Dommy Laughton's room and went down the stairs two at a time. It was dark there, and he cursed the darkness as he blundered through it. When he got near the front door the door quivered open and a screeching shape staggered out.

Peter got both hands on the man's shoulders and stopped him, straight-armed him against the wall. Enough light blurred through the open door to lessen the murk in the corridor and reveal Deemer's face, convulsed with terror and shiny wet with rain. The eyes were enormous, and the gaping mouth struggled horribly to empty itself of sound.

"What's the matter?" Peter bellowed. "What happened?"

Deemer spewed terror-noises that weren't words, didn't make sense. But the name Unwin was among them, and Peter remembered that a man by that name had been in the kitchen of the inn when he and Jo had first arrived.

"Out there!" Deemer wailed. "Out there in the street! He's all twisted and—"

Peter didn't get the rest. His pounding feet made thunder to the doorway and he charged down the veranda steps. Gulping cold, damp air into his lungs, he rushed into the street, ploughed through the misty yellow glow under a street lamp and went past looming shadow-shapes that were stores, and saw something crawling.

Crawling . . .

IT was dark here, and the shape was a human thing wriggling sluggishly along the ground. Moaning. Moaning horribly. And crawling in agony toward the hotel.

Dark, but not so dark that Peter's horrified eyes missed any of the ghastly details. Not so dark that those twisted arms and legs, that contorted body, were hidden from his gaping eyes. Swaying on stiff legs, he stared and then jerked forward slowly, fighting a frantic desire to turn and run. And the thing kept crawling, without seeing him.

Tom Unwin. A little while ago the man had been sitting in the kitchen of the inn. Normal then. Now he was like the husband of that mad woman in the farmhouse. Now he was one of the twisted ones.

Peter hunched over him and hooked both arms under him and picked him up. It took courage to do that. This hellish disease might be contagious.

Peter picked him up and carried him and went stumbling back to the veranda where Josiah Deemer stood staring in abject terror. Peter lurched up the steps and went past Deemer and lugged that moaning, twisted shape inside. Deemer blundered after him.

Terror was a vile, monstrous, devouring parasite in Deemer's brain, glazing his eyes and pushing uncouth sounds out of his wet mouth.

Jo, coming downstairs, looked at the thing in Peter's arms and tried to stifle a shriek. Peter carried that twisted thing into the kitchen and lowered it onto a couch. "Damn you, Deemer, snap out of it! Go for a doctor!"

"I sent the doctor out to Bert Crandall's house," Deemer blubbered. "He'll be gone there now. I was com-

Peter swayed around and stared

in' back from his place when I seen Tom in the street, crawlin' . . ." The words trailed off. "It won't do no good to get the doctor. He couldn't help the others. Tom's the fourth now . . ."

Peter groaned. God, what could you do? It was wrong to stand there staring while a human being writhed in such fearsome agony, but what could you *do?* No medicine could straighten those crooked limbs or make that brain normal again. The merciful thing would be a bullet.

Jo did things. Got water and towels and bathed the man's face, wiping away blood and dirt. Peter sat down and looked at the floor and raised his head after a long while to say dully: "How did it happen, Deemer?"

"I don't know. I was comin' back from the doctor's place and I seen him crawlin' in the street."

"That's all you know?"

"I know who's responsible for it! Klinger!"

"Peter, come here," Jo said from the couch. "I think he—I think it's all over. He's not breathing."

A little while later, Jo and Peter went silently upstairs again, and the thing in the kitchen lay with a blanket pulled over it. Jo's face was white and drawn; her eyes burned too brightly in sunken sockets.

Rain drummed hollowly on a creaking roof, and there were other night-noises accompanied by the wheeze of Peter's labored breathing. The door of Dommy Laughton's room was closed; the door of their own room hung ajar, and Jo had left a light burning. Something white gleamed on the threshold.

Jo picked it up, frowning. It was an oblong of paper with words on it. She handed it to Peter and he held it in a big, stiff hand that twitched a little. The penciled words said:

> The twisted ones are now four in number. If you are fools enough to buy the Klinger estate, two more will join the brotherhood of broken men! Leave here before it is too late! It is death to defy Endren Klinger!

Peter read the words and made growling sounds in his throat and crumpled the paper savagely. A mistake, that note. Jo, knowing Peter as only a wife can know her husband, could have told the writer that her man was the kind who could be coaxed but not commanded.

Peter narrowed his eyes ominously and glared at his wife. "So we're to be added to the list, are we? We're being ordered out of here. All right, pal, we'll stay. And tomorrow we'll get a look at this Klinger place, and maybe we'll buy it. Maybe we'll even do that!"

CHAPTER III
The Thing in the Box

MR. RUSSEL POLK, the lawyer, said in his purring voice: "And this is the house itself."

The rain of last night had let up an hour ago. Sunlight was struggling to eat through a sky filled with sluggish, low-hanging clouds. In that murky light, half mist and half sun, the home of Endren Klinger seemed strangely dark and aloof and repelling. It looked, Peter thought, like some kind of asylum.

He and Jo had left the inn without waiting for Deemer to get breakfast. The man had been in no condition to get breakfast anyway, after a sleepless night of terror. Peter and Jo had gone to Polk's house. And now, three miles out of town on the old back road that twisted through the valley, Polk was fumbling with keys and opening the front door of the abandoned Klinger place, and was standing aside with that waxen smile on his face.

Peter, eyeing him critically, wondered how Jo could ever have been a close friend of the man. Jo had been. "Yes," she had admitted, when Peter had spoken to her about the tactless outburst of Josiah Deemer, "he—he wanted to marry me."

Maybe Polk hadn't grown that waxen smile then. It hung on the man's face like something smeared on the face of a subway poster, ugly and artificial. Other than that, Polk would probably be considered good-looking. But the smile worked on Peter's nerves.

Or perhaps it was the atmosphere of this gloomy house, where rain-swelled timbers creaked to every footstep, and great hulks of furniture devoured all the space in low-ceilinged rooms.

"A remarkable house in some ways," Polk was saying. "Klinger admired antiques. These carpets, you'll notice, are ancient Persians ..."

"It gives me the creeps!" Jo said.

"But you do like the house itself?"

"Of course!"

Later, Peter signed papers and wrote out a check. And when that was done, Polk said quietly: "I imagine you're rather curious about the man who lived here."

Jo nodded.

"The story that is going the rounds," Polk shrugged, "is largely an exaggeration. Of course, Klinger *was* disliked because of his eccentricities, and the villagers did order him to leave Greendon. But he really left because of the treatment he was receiving. When he had stood all he could, he put his affairs into my hands and gave me full authority to sell this house and all in it, just as it stands.

"He named his price and promised to return at some later date to collect it. The villagers"—again that waxen smile came out of Polk's pale cheeks —"seem to think he has returned already, for evil reasons. That's nonsense, of course."

"Yes," Jo said. "That's nonsense— of course."

"You and your husband will live here?"

"We'll live here"—Jo's voice was strangely vibrant, stirring echoes in the shadowed corners of the room— "while we make arrangements to have the place renovated. Yes."

The waxen smile was still on Polk's face when he left.

Peter stretched himself in a musty chair and peered around him, scowling. It would take a long while, he thought, to take the morguelike atmosphere out of this place. All this hoary furniture would have to be heaved out; the grotesque lighting fixtures would have to come down. A thousand and one things. . . .

"Peter—"

"Yes, Jo?"

"You're not angry with me?"

His scowl vanished. "Angry? If the joint's okay with you, honey, it suits me."

They went from room to room, he and Jo, together. They explored musty closets, small, damp chambers which contained enormous collections of junk. Upstairs and down, even to attic and cellar. In one room Peter stood, hands on hips, before a portrait of Endren Klinger and peered critically into close-set eyes that seemed to stare back at him.

"Not a bad-looking cuss," he mused. "About sixty, maybe a bit more. Intelligent, sort of aloof, probably a man who never made friends easily."

"I wonder," Jo said queerly, "where he is now and what he's doing."

Peter glanced sharply at her, but the worried look went out of her face before he was even certain it had existed. "I'm going upstairs," Jo said, "and do what I can to make one of the bedrooms less cobwebby. Coming?"

He shook his head. When she had left him, he went through the kitchen and down a crooked flight of stairs to the cellar. It was dark down there. Something on four legs scurried across the concrete floor and made whispering sounds along the wall. Peter stood stiff, listening, then went forward again.

Someone — or something — was watching him. Watching every move he made. He felt it. "Nerves," he muttered.

But he knew better. His nerves had never gone back on him before. This was a tangible, unpleasant sensation that crept into him and festered in his brain. He wasn't afraid of it, exactly. It angered him.

HE stopped again and made fists of his big hands and glared around him, silently challenging the owner of those invisible, malignant eyes to step out of the gloom and make a fight of it. Rage pushed a snarl to his lips. But there was no movement in the shadows, no vaguest sound. . . .

Sullenly alert, he paced into deeper darkness, past the looming hulk of a huge furnace, past the high wooden wall of a coal-bin. It was a big cellar. Too big. And like the rooms in the house above, it was a weird world of twilight and unsavory silence. A morgue.

Those invisible eyes were still watching.

Twice he jerked around, positive that someone was dogging his steps. Then, grimly defiant, he struck matches and explored the gloomy recesses on both sides of him, and invaded storerooms choked with furniture.

Standing in the doorway of one storeroom, he held a sputtering match between thumb and forefinger and stared at a long, pinewood box that resembled a coffin. It wasn't a coffin; it was a packing-case, probably had held some of Klinger's antiques. But he went stiffly toward it, scowling, and dragged a couple of other boxes off the top of it, and stooped to lift the cover.

The match scorched the ball of his thumb and he dropped it, grumbling. Straightening, he fumbled for another and found one, and reached down to scratch it on the cover of the packing-case that resembled a coffin.

Behind him in the doorway a low voice said softly: "It is death to touch that. Be careful!"

Peter Smith used a lot of time in turning. The muscles of his big body had stiffened; his heart was pounding and he was holding his breath. Like a stuffed dummy on a store-window turntable he swayed around, and straightened. And stared.

Because he was a man whose emotions worked slowly, he didn't cry out. He just stood there, both arms hooked in front of him. After a while he said grimly:

"Klinger!"

"Yes, I am Endren Klinger."

Peter put a twitching hand to his face and pawed the bulging muscles of his jaw. Like a drunken man gaping at something inconceivable, he was slow to believe in the reality of what he stared at. The doorway was dark. The intruder was a gaunt black shape standing in the murk.

Only the face was really visible. The face was dead. It belonged on a corpse.

Peter took a faltering step backward, stopped when his left foot made a hollow thumping sound against the packing-case. His hands were fists. He sucked breath through his teeth and not once did he shift his gaze from the cadaverous face in the doorway.

Not once did the eyes in that spectral death-mask cease studying him.

The man who stood there was Endren Klinger. There was no mistake about that. Death had caused those blackened cheeks to recede against a protruding framework of bone, and decay had eaten the flesh-pits in which those glowing eyes were imbedded. Death had made a thin, gaunt, skeletal shape of the dangling body under that black shroud. But the man was surely Endren Klinger.

"So you've come back," Peter said slowly, pulling the words through a bloated thickness in his throat, "for revenge . . ."

There was no answer. He hadn't expected an answer. For that matter he wasn't conscious of the words that croaked from his own lips. He took a heavy step forward, and another. From out of the voluminous folds of the black robe a rotted, shrunken hand stabbed toward him.

"Stand where you are."

Peter's thick legs stiffened under him.

"Now hear what I have to say," Klinger commanded. "This house is mine, and I have returned to dwell in it. With you and your wife I have no quarrel, but you must leave here at once and forever. Do you understand?"

Dead lips, talking. But they were uttering words, and that was proof enough that they could feel the crushing impact of a clenched fist. "I'll see you in hell!" Peter Smith snarled.

HE lunged. The distance was not great, and he went in a headlong rush, shoulders hunched, legs driving. The thing in the doorway moved sideward with the gliding rapidity of a monstrous snake. Head down, Peter hurtled through the aperture, through the space where that macaber monster had loomed.

A grinding weight met the side of his head, hurled him sprawling. Agony roared through him, eating its way through skull and brain and burning down into his big chest. He crashed to the floor with both arms doubled under him, one knee hooked into the pit of his stomach.

Blood was gushing from his face. Hot blood, burning as it ran into his eyes. And the spectral face above him was receding slowly into darkness, into a pulsing, screaming darkness that descended amid grinding thunder to engulf him. . . .

He wondered, some time later, how long he had lain unconscious. It was hard to tell. Blood was still warm and wet on his face, and there was a vast, throbbing ache that went on and on, relentlessly.

"Jo!" he mumbled. "Please—Jo—" But Jo would be upstairs in one of the bedrooms. She wouldn't know what had happened. He had to get on his feet and go up there and tell her. She mustn't stay in this house any longer. Not with Klinger come back from the dead. . . .

She mustn't stay here . . . Strange, the pictures his warped brain dragged into being. There was Josiah Deemer talking in a shrill voice, about Russel Polk having once been sweet on Jo. And twisted men crawling, and a mad woman screeching curses. And an oblong box that looked like a coffin.

Jo mustn't stay here. It was dangerous.

He went upstairs and found her in one of the bedrooms. "We're getting out of here," he said. And she stared at him, her eyes wide with sudden terror.

"Peter! What's happened to you? There's blood—!"

"Tell you later. We haven't time now. Come!"

When she saw the grim, hard scowl on his face she did not protest. Together they walked out of the room and down the hall to the head of the stairs, Peter striding stiff and straight, Jo stumbling a little, clinging to her husband's arm.

Man and woman, abandoning their home because a macaber monster from the grave had threatened them with annihilation. But there was nothing ignoble in that exodus. Peter's head was high, his eyes smoldering. When he had removed his wife to a place of safety he would come back.

He opened the door. In the driveway a dust-covered sedan was disgorging muttering men, and the men were tramping toward the veranda steps. Josiah Deemer led the procession. Behind him came Russel Polk, the lawyer who had once wanted Jo's hand in marriage.

Peter stood scowling.

"What are they coming here for?" Jo said in bewilderment. And then the muttering men ascended the steps and pushed forward, and Josiah Deemer said in a shrill, nervous voice: "We've found out something, Mr. Smith! We've discovered the truth about Endren Klinger!"

Peter's hand went out and gripped Jo's arm. He peered into the grim, determined faces before him.

"So have I," he said in a voice that barely crept beyond his curled lips. "Come in—and we'll talk."

It was a strange gathering. Men sat in ugly overstuffed chairs and peered uneasily about them, fearing the shadows that hung beyond the ochre glow of dusty lamps. Men stared at Jo, because a woman in that grim gathering seemed out of place.

"THIS is Furstin Adams," Josiah Deemer said. "He runs the Adams Huntin' Camps over to Moon Lake."

Peter gazed with narrowed eyes at the man indicated by Deemer's jerking thumb. A small man, garbed in woodsman's breeches, hunting boots, a man with furtive, restless eyes that roamed like frightened beetles in their sockets. Adams was afraid of something.

"You tell Smith what you told us," Russel Polk said.

Adams wriggled in his chair. "Well, it goes back a couple of months. Back to a day when Endren Klinger wrote me and four other men to come here to this house and talk with him about something. I'm the only one of that group still living. The others are all—dead."

"The twisted ones," Deemer muttered. "Crandall and Unwin and the others."

"Klinger got us here that night and he says: 'Gentlemen, as you know, I am a retired professor of physics and I have lived here alone with my studies for a good many years. During that time,' he says, 'I have worked on a formula for poison-gas control which will revolutionize all current theories of war defense. My invention is worth money. But,' he says, 'I need money to perfect it before I can bargain with the government.' "

Adams put out a thick, coated tongue and lapped at his lips. "Well, Klinger had it all worked out. If we was interested in making a good-size fortune for ourselves, we had to each give him a thousand dollars. In return he'd give us each a copy of this formula of his which was a long mess of figures that used up 'most ten typewritten pages.

"We was each to get a copy, and the copies would be all alike. Mind you, the stuff he gave us wasn't complete. He himself was the only man in possession of the whole formula. But he done it that way so none of us could go ahead and cheat the others, or cheat him. On the other hand, he wouldn't be able to cheat us, because if he tried it, we'd be in possession of enough of his data to ruin him.

"Well, he left us alone in this room and we talked it over, and we figured it was a pretty fair investment."

"And"—Josiah Deemer was leaning forward, peering into Adams' face—"you gave him the money?"

"Yes, we done that. And then the people of Greendon got down on Klinger and run him out of town. And then"—Adams made a rattling noise with his teeth—"the five men who gave Klinger that money begun to die off, one by one. . . ."

NO one answered. Peter glanced at his wife and curled his lips in a hard scowl. Russell Polk put a cigarette to his mouth and scratched a match on the uplifted sole of his shoe. The crackling of the match was sudden thunder in the room's strained silence.

"So you're the last of the five," Peter said grimly, peering at Adams, "and you're afraid."

"Of course I'm afraid! Who wouldn't be?"

"And you believe that Klinger, after bargaining for the money he needed, deliberately murdered four men to get back the papers he gave for security?"

"That's what I believe," Adams mumbled.

"Then why did you come here and tell *me?*" demanded Peter Smith.

"We didn't come to tell you," Polk said quietly. "We came to find Klinger. It stands to reason that if the man returned to carry out his murder-campaign, he is hiding here somewhere in this house which he built himself."

"And you want to search the place?"

"We do."

Peter pushed himself up. "It's a big house. A man could easily hide himself here." He could have said more. Could have told them that this house of evil *was* the hiding-place of the man they sought. But that would have called for detailed explanations, and there were things that could not rationally be explained away.

The men of Greendon, muttering among themselves, were already moving from the room. Russell Polk led the search, and a look of fear was smeared now on Polk's face. These men were afraid. They feared the thing they were seeking.

They went plodding through musty rooms and gloomy corridors, upstairs first, then through the labyrinth of chambers on the lower level, grimly probing every shadowed retreat, every possible place of concealment. Then the cellar. The cellar where a corpse-faced creature, walking in decay, had clubbed Peter Smith unconscious.

"There's a storeroom here," Peter said, "with a box in it."

This time he would open that box and learn the truth.

They trailed him to the storeroom, Polk scowling unpleasantly because the leadership of the party had fallen suddenly on Peter Smith's shoulders. Already the gloom of the cellar had worked on the men's nerves. Josiah Deemer was peering fearfully into murky corners. Furstin Adams, who perhaps had more reason to be afraid than did any of the others, kept dabbing a drenched handkerchief at his wet face.

Peter, scowling with memories of what had happened here, strode ahead of the group and stood beside the pinewood box that so resembled a coffin. Jo came to his side, frowning, Furstin Adams, terrified, moved back to the doorway.

"There's something in this box," Peter muttered. "Something that Klinger doesn't want us to find." His big hand, reaching down, was stiff and white in the gleam of a searchlight held by Deemer. His fingers fastened on the lid.

The lid was nailed down. Peter braced a foot against the box and used both hands, pulled steadily. Nails groaned in the fibrous wood. The cover cracked back.

PETER gaped with horror-filled eyes and stepped back, slowly, against the men who crowded forward. Deemer screamed. Jo screamed, too, and bottled the sound in her throat before it could pursue the echoes of Deemer's shrill outburst through the cellar.

The thing in the pinewood box was dead. It had been dead for days, perhaps weeks. A strangling odor of decay rose from it like swamp-mist, gagging the men who stared.

Angular features, rotted and disintegrating, leered horribly in the glow of Deemer's searchlight. A cavernous maw of mouth was grinning. In those staring, eyeless sockets alien white things were crawling and feeding.

Yet the features were recognizable. The dead thing in the box was Endren Klinger!

Belief in the supernatural comes hard to some men. It sledged its way remorselessly into Peter's sluggish brain and gnawed there, eating deeper, battering down his resistance. He stood swaying, his big hands opening and closing convulsively.

Endren Klinger, *here?* No! This rotted horror in the box must be the corpse of someone else. It *couldn't* be Klinger! But—

He stopped t h i n k i n g. D o w n through floors and ceiling in the house above shrilled a mad clamor that wailed eerily into the death chamber. Up there someone was shrieking in terror and torment. The men of Greendon stopped muttering

among themselves, stiffened a n d stood listening. One of them cried hoarsely: "My God, what's that?"

"It must be Adams!" Jo said fearfully. "He's not here with us!"

Peter was first to make thunder on the cellar stairs. The others followed, leaving behind the pinewood box and its grisly occupant. Bellowing Adams' name, Peter fumed through the kitchen, along the dim corridor to the front of the house. Headlong he charged into the livingroom, and stopped.

Furstin Adams was no longer screaming.

Adams would never scream again. He lay across the legs of an antique table, his arms twined around the table-legs, his body humped and contorted and horrible.

An expression of intense agony still lingered on the man's frozen face. But he was not in agony now. He never would be again.

The curse had caught him. "He came up here alone," Peter mumbled, pacing forward. "He was afraid of what we might find when we opened the box. . . ." And it was as though giant hands had seized Adams' body and crushed it, bent it out of shape.

Jo clung to Peter's arm and the men of Greendon pushed forward to stare. Terrified, all of them.

"But who did it?" Deemer whimpered. "Who could have done it? Klinger is dead. . . ."

Peter shook his head. "Klinger's not dead."

They gaped at him. Was *he* going mad now?

"Klinger's not dead!" Peter roared. "I know what I'm saying. That thing down there has the power to come prowling out of its coffin! It's horribly alive!"

The men of Greendon shrank from him, and Jo's eyes widened with amazement. But he stood there, fists clenched at his sides, and defied them. "The corpse of Endren Klinger is not dead!"

They were afraid of him then. Even Jo moved away, trembling. Jo said, "No, dear God, no!" and Peter growled his defiance. Somehow Jo found courage enough to come forward and put a hand on his arm. "Peter, dear, you mustn't—"

That was a mistake. Had she stood with him in his sullen rage, she might later have soothed him into submission, led him out of this house where danger lurked. But to plead with him and show that she too was afraid —that was wrong.

"Get out!" he roared. "This is my house and I'm ordering you out of it, the whole damned muttering lot of you! Take Furstin Adams with you and take my wife back to the village where she'll be safe. I'm staying here!"

"No, Peter. I won't go!"

He glared at her. The first time in his life he had ever done that, or ever became angry with her. "You'll go if I have to throw you out!" he snarled.

And Jo went with the others. Sobbing wretchedly, not knowing what best to do, she let them lead her over the threshold. Peter stood in the hall, cursing them as the door thudded shut.

CHAPTER IV
Liquid Death

HIS rage was a long time subsiding, and then, realizing what he had done, he was bewildered. Why had he been so angry?

He sat in the living-room and stared around him. Funny, how much emptier the place seemed with Jo gone. Why had he lost his temper?

But there was something he had to do now, something he *must* do in order to prove to the others, and to himself, that he was not mad. That thing downstairs in the coffin. . . .

He paced slowly down the hall. Rain was whispering again at shut windows, pounding a dirge on the roof. The house itself was strangely still. Too still. The shadows were deeper.

Vaguely afraid, he descended into the cellar and entered the storeroom where the corpse of Endren Klinger

lay rotting. Josiah Deemer's searchlight lay there on the floor where Deemer had dropped it. Peter scooped it up. And the corpse still lay in its coffin, with white, wriggling things feeding in blackened flesh.

He looked down on it. "It's still here. It has been dead a long time, and yet I saw it walking and heard the sound of its voice." Thoughts like that, gnawing at a man's brain, can devour his reason. And those thoughts spawned others.

"Before I search the house I'll make sure he *stays* here. I'll nail the coffin shut again!"

Later he went back upstairs, muttering: "They think I'm mad, but by God, I'll show them! I'll *make* them believe!"

Rain drummed against shut windows as he went wandering through musty chambers which had already been explored by the men of Greendon. Damp timbers creaked underfoot, mocking him, and he was a strange, stiff figure, sometimes silent, sometimes mumbling to himself, always staring with dark, smoldering eyes in which anger still burned.

Downstairs the front door groaned open, swung shut with a reverberating thud. Peter stood stiff, listening.

Someone had come into the house. Someone down there was walking with quick, nervous steps along the corridor. Then: "Peter, where are you?" And it was Jo's voice, laden with anxiety. Jo had returned!

Peter strode over the bedroom threshold and along the hall to the head of the stairs. Jo's voice came again, shrilly, calling his name—and suddenly the voice was strangled in a scream of terror that shrilled wildly up the stair-well. Peter again heard sounds of conflict!

He went stumbling forward, both arms pushed out ahead of him. The sounds ceased before he got to the stairhead. He blundered down, bellowing Jo's name, went off balance and caught himself, lurched blindly along the lower hall.

Jo wasn't there. Nothing was there.

He stood swaying, pawing the wall.

"Jo! Oh God, Jo!" No answer to that. Nothing but the rattling sob of his own breathing and the mutter of the rain. And an empty corridor where Jo had screamed and fought and been dragged away.

She had come back, seeking him, and that death faced monster of darkness had been lying in wait to seize her. Now she was gone!

Peter blundered forward. Life had seeped out of his body, left him a stumbling, half-animate clod without a brain. He couldn't think now. His skull was full of a single annihilating thought, and the thought numbed him. Jo. . . .

He went through the labyrinth of rooms, sobbing her name, peering hopelessly into shadows. When he came at last to the dark stairs leading down into the cellar he might not have descended, might have turned and lumbered back to the front of the house if the cellar's gloom had not vomited forth a wailing cry of anguish that jerked him forward.

He lurched down the stairs and stood swaying at the bottom. The scream came again, from the end of the cellar where that nailed coffin lay in a musty storeroom. He went toward it. No searchlight now. Nothing to show him the way. Only Jo's voice, moaning, and another voice snarling unintelligible words.

The storeroom door was closed. He thudded against it, got his hands on the knob and strove in vain to wrench the barrier open. Locked. "Jo! The door's locked!" He hurled himself against it, and when he fell back, gasping for breath, the sounds from within had ceased. There was another sound in the murk behind him. A whisper of stalking feet.

He lurched around, jammed his back hard against the door as the darkness rushed toward him. No, it wasn't darkness, it was something black and horrible *in* the dark. Something with a rotted, cadaverous face and twisted hands, and the hands were curled around a bludgeon, and the bludgeon was whining down through space.

Peter had no time even to push his arms under the blow. The weapon crashed with the force of a swung sledge. He groaned, and the groan went with him, gutturally, into a world of darkness. . . .

"SO you won't tell. You'd rather die and take your secret to the grave." Funny how thin and shrill that voice was. How like a knife reaching into the core of his twisted soul. "Very well, I'll *force* you to tell!"

The voice came through crowding darkness, and the darkness itself was sluggishly breaking apart, thinning to a dull grey mist of pain. Through it came shafts of yellow lantern light.

"I warn you, you'll talk before I'm finished! There are ways of making a woman talk!"

"But I don't know! How can I tell you what I don't *know?*"

The voices echoed in his brain, as though riding the shafts of ochre light that burned against his eyes. Something had happened a little while ago. A descending bludgeon. . . .

The agony-mist cleared slowly and Peter Smith groaned, opened his bloodshot eyes. This was the storeroom, and he lay with his shoulders jammed against the coffin which had contained Klinger's corpse. The door was closed and a dangling lantern glowed against the opposite wall. And the corpse wasn't in the coffin. It stood there, dark and evil and hideous, near the door. Endren Klinger, risen from the dead. . . .

Peter turned his head toward the voices. It hurt him to move, hurt him even to hunch himself higher against the box. Blood was hot against his swollen lips. But he stared.

A woman stood there against the wall, in the glare of the lantern. Peter Smith's wife, bound in a tangle of ropes, her face white and rigid. Only in the eyes was there life left. The eyes stared—not at Peter, but at a creature who crouched there before her.

"Think, my dear," the creature was

saying. "For the sake of a few filthy dollars you are condemning yourself and your husband to death. You are a fool!"

Jo shook her head. "No, no! I don't *know* where Klinger's papers are!"

"But I am sure you do. That's why you bought Klinger's house—returned to Greendon." The voice had purring qualities now, as if striving to drug her terrified brain. "Listen to me. With the help of my noble assistant I have slain six men—Klinger and his five associates. I have been put to a great deal of trouble. It was necessary, first of all, to turn the people of Greendon against Klinger, so that they would order him out of town—so that he, in turn, would become violently angry and threaten them. Then it was necessary to destroy him, and to do it in such a manner that the people of Greendon would think he had quietly left town.

"All this trouble I have been through, in order to gain possession of Klinger's formula and to destroy those men with whom he partially shared his secret, and to commit those murders in such a manner that Klinger would be blamed for them. You must realize, my dear, that *your* life and that of your husband mean very little to me after what I have already accomplished!"

Strange, how familiar that purring voice was! Peter, struggling to remember many things, knew that he had heard it before and tried hard to put a name to it. But this was no time to gnaw at details. Jo was in trouble!

Painfully he pushed himself higher and sucked breath into his aching chest. Strength was dribbling back into his battered body. If he could stand up. . . .

"Be careful, Peter Smith! If you move too much, it means death!"

He jerked his head toward the threat. *That* voice was familiar, too. Once before it had snarled at him in this same dark room of madness. He glared into the cadaverous face of the corpse-creature who stood near the door, watching him. Klinger's corpse. And one of those rotted hands held a pistol. This monster was the other man's assistant. . . .

Peter turned again to peer at the creature who stood near Jo. "So you see," the fellow was saying viciously, "I have destroyed many lives in order to acquire Klinger's secret. And I *have* acquired it, all except the part which Klinger himself retained. Those papers were hidden somewhere in this house when he met his death. I looked for them in vain.

"At first I thought that your interest in this house was a mere coincidence. I ordered my assistant to frighten you into leaving. But now I realize the truth. *You* know where the papers are!"

"Dear God," Jo moaned, "I tell you I know nothing about it!"

"I am convinced that you do." The gaze of those narrowed eyes fastened evilly on Jo's frozen features. "And I am giving you one last chance to talk, before I use *this!*"

A glass-bellied hypodermic needle darted toward Jo's stomach. Peter, staring with eyes that threatened to burst in their sockets, saw a white liquid lapping the inner walls of the tube.

"This, my dear, is what turned Greendon into a place of twisted men. My good assistant, Doctor Glending, invented it." The evil face swung slowly to leer at the monster near the door. "You see, when I planned this campaign of mine I went to Glending and demanded his help. And he gave it to me because he feared to do otherwise. If I were to uncover his past, I could solve an ugly mystery for the police and send him to prison for life, for murder."

THERE was something druglike in that droning voice. Something vile that crept into Peter's brain and numbed him. He stared, could do nothing else. "The serum in this syringe, my dear, will take you to hell. If I give you enough of it, it will destroy you almost instantly, as it destroyed Furstin Adams. Now will you tell me what I want to know? Choose. Either tell me, or—"

"I don't *know!* My God, Dommy, I swear it!"

Dommy. The name stuck in Peter's brain, meant something. He had heard it before, at the Greendon Inn. Dommy. Dommy Laughton, Josiah Deemer's orphaned nephew!

And now Dommy's voice was shrill with menace. "So you refuse to talk. Very well, perhaps your tongue will loosen a little when you see your husband writhing in agony. We'll see."

He paced forward, and Peter Smith stared at him in sudden horror. The thing had not been real before. It had been some strange drama in which he, Peter Smith, had been only a bewildered spectator. Now the drama had spilled over into the audience and was hellishly personal.

The twisted men! He, Peter Smith, was to become one of them, was to shriek in agony as the serum in that glass ran through his veins.

"Get back!" he bellowed. "By God, you can't do it! You can't!"

The leering face of Dommy Laughton grew larger as it floated toward him. "Oh, yes, I can. If he moves, Glending, shoot him. Shoot to kill."

Terror fumed in Peter's big body, strangling him. This was the end. Dear God, it mustn't be! Jo was over there, staring with enormous eyes and moaning in a voice that welled from the depths of a soul torn with anguish. His Jo! What would become of her?

Dommy Laughton came closer. Near the door his assistant stood stiff, holding a gun that would belch death. Peter stared wildly from one to the other, from Dommy's twisted face to the death-mask of the man who under Dommy's direction had masqueraded as the resurrected corpse of Endren Klinger, so that the superstitious folk of Greendon, if they encountered him, would still blame Klinger—or the thing which had been Klinger—for the horrors in their midst.

Doctor Glending had entered into this thing unwillingly. Men had died in agony from the effects of the hellish serum he had created, but he had not wanted to create that serum. If

Glending were faced now with the task of murdering a man, would he hesitate?

It was Peter Smith's only hope. He tensed himself. Hands flat on the floor, legs stiffened for a superhuman effort, he waited—and then hurled himself headlong at his advancing assailant.

GLENDING uttered a cry of dismay and jerked the gun higher, but fired a fraction of a second too late. The bullet missed its mark.

Peter Smith stormed head-foremost into the creature before him. With all the strength in his big arms he lifted Dommy Laughton from the floor and hurled him, flung him straight at Glending's rigid body. The gun in Glending's fist roared again, and Dommy Laughton screamed. And then, snarling, Peter fell upon the cringing form of Dommy's assistant and dragged the man down.

It was no battle. On his knees, with Glending's writhing body beneath him, Peter leaned on corded arms and seized the doctor's throat. Rage had doubled the strength in his big hands, and the hands retained their grip until Glending's writhing body became still. They didn't kill. They could have, but didn't.

Suddenly, behind Peter, a woman was screaming.

He lurched sideward just in time, whirled and spun clear of the glass-bellied syringe that stabbed toward him. The hand holding the syringe was bloody; the retching face behind it was a mask of bubbling crimson. Glending's second bullet had done that. Aimed at Peter, the bullet had buried itself in Dommy Laughton's face. This murderous threat of the needle was a final effort to turn the tables.

It failed. Peter's fist crashed with sledge-hammer force, and Dommy collapsed, rolled over in a twisted, hideous heap. The bullet had done its work.

"We're getting out of here, Jo." Peter said that twice, and was mumbling it a third time as he released his wife. "Come on—we're leaving." He picked up the unbroken death-syringe as he led her to the door.

The death-syringe. The creator of twisted men. . . .

AS I said before, I could have made this more personal. I could have given Peter Smith his right name and Jo hers. But some of you might start at me and—well, some of you might not try to understand.

But there are newspaper stories of those frightful days when Greendon was a place of twisted men. There are men in Greendon, today, who will tell you what they know. There are newspaper records of the trial and conviction and hanging of Doctor Paul Glending for a murder committed in 1907, to which he confessed.

The serum in that glass-bellied syringe was analyzed by a State expert, whose report went something like this:

> This serum seems to be one hitherto unknown. I would say that its basic content is a pathogenic virus capable of producing effects paralleling the symptoms of acute poliomyelitis. Glending, having entry to several large hospitals, may have obtained the basic ingredient for his serum from the spinal fluid of persons afflicted with acute and complicated forms of paralysis.

I am quite certain that this serum, if injected into the blood stream in even a minute quantity, would produce not only instantaneous imbecility, thus rendering the victim incapable of remembering what had happened to him, but would result also in rapid macromelus of the organs, malformation of the bones, and ultimate death. The speed of death would depend on the amount of virus injected.

The same State expert, after assisting at an autopsy of Dommy Laughton's bullet-shattered corpse, reported, if I remember correctly:

> It is apparent that Laughton suffered from periodic mental incapacity, or ideophrenic insanity, caused perhaps by chronic melancholy. . . .

As for Klinger's secret, you may believe what you like. His house was searched; most of it was dismantled in the process. Perhaps there are papers hidden somewhere which, if combined with those for which Dommy Laughton committed murder, might be worth a vast amount of money. Perhaps—and I think this more probable — those undiscovered formulae remained locked in Klinger's brain when he went to his death.

I don't particularly care. Jo and Peter Smith have each other. . . .

BLOOD FOR THE WOLF-PACK

A clutching hand of horror closed over Hal Cleaves' heart

Howling Timber Creatures Skulking Through the Snow-Covered Woods Act as a Background for Human Beasts That Terrorize a French Canadian Village!

By HUGH B. CAVE

Author of "The Twisted Men," "Hell's Darkest Halls," etc.

"FIVE years ago tonight—"

In Darnell's musty living room, Hal Cleaves stared with narrowed eyes at the photograph on the ancient mahogany table. As photographs went, it wasn't much—merely an enlarged, poorly colored snapshot. But Dessein was a small village of but two hundred inhabitants, sunk deep in the Canadian wilderness, and undoubtedly this was mail order work from Quebec.

She was a striking woman, the creature in the picture. Raven hair, large dark eyes, lips made to be kissed—yes she was beautiful! The mother of poor young feeble-minded Paul Darnell. Five years ago tonight she had vanished, leaving her husband and nine-year-old son behind.

For five years, Pierre Darnell had lived in a world of shadows, waiting without hope for her to return. A world that was becoming almost as deep and dark as that into which his son had been plunged at an early age.

Something about the face in the photograph was disturbingly familiar. It worked on Hal Cleaves' mind, troubled him. Had he seen that face before somewhere?

Nonsense! Never before in his life had he been within a thousand miles of this isolated village. Not until last winter, when Virginia had come to Dessein to take charge of the rural school, had he even known that such a place existed.

Yet the face troubled him. There was something about it — something haunting, that refused to be forgotten. Just as there was, in this musty old house, an ever-present miasma of impending sorrow, a vibration, a *feeling* that something had to happen. From the very beginning he'd been aware of it.

Eleven o'clock. The old clock on the fireplace mantel was whispering out the hour, like an old woman mumbling over her beads. How still the house was! Pierre had gone to bed hours ago. Virginia was upstairs, reading to the invalid sister. It was so damnably lonely here, so cold!

Cleaves put aside the book he was reading and paced silently to a window, stood there looking out at the moon-washed carpet of deep snow which ran for miles to the north. A light glowed in the small apartment over the barn, where Lemming, the caretaker, slept. But there was no sound, no life, in the white night.

No wonder Virginia wanted to get away from here. No wonder she had begged him to drive up from Boston, marry her, take her home. A year in this gloomy old house could drive a normal human being insane!

And what was that Virginia had written? Something about werewolves —the mutterings of the superstitious villagers. A few children had been found recently, mangled, bloody, their frail bodies twisted and gnawed almost beyond recognition. Wolves—yes, it might have been wolves, the dread of the simple *habitants*. But—but it might be a werewolf, a creature of another kind menacing them—a creature of another kind—like the school teacher!

Cleaves laughed, and then checked himself. Virginia was taking it seriously, after all—and you never could tell what a clannish group of townspeople would do.

Hoping that the door of the sister's room would be open, so he could motion Virginia into the hall for a good night kiss, Cleaves slowly climbed the carpeted stairs. But the door was shut.

He paused for a moment, listening to the drone of Virginia's voice. Queer stuff she was reading. Stuff about spiritualism—a subject in which Anne, Pierre's invalid sister, was darkly interested. With a sigh, Cleaves went down the hall to his own room.

Something would happen soon. Something *had* to happen! Those were his thoughts as he dropped off to sleep.

When he awoke, the wolves were howling in the white waste beyond the village. Their mournful cries sent a shudder through him. But it was not the wolves that had awakened him. There was something else, closer, here in the house!

A woman—shrieking!

The sound was like a magnet, so close that Cleaves felt the sucking strength of it dragging him out of bed. His bare feet slapped the floor, slid into the slippers that lay there. He pushed his arms into the sleeves of his dressing-gown and flung open the door.

NO sound now. No sound after that first agony-laden scream, from the room at the end of the hall. Anne's room! Dear God, perhaps *Virginia* had screamed! Gin had been in there, reading!

He raced down the hall, but was not the first to reach that open door. Pierre Darnell, grey-haired and frail and gasping, came padding around the bend of the corridor ahead of him. Pierre's bony hands clutched the door frame. His lean body swayed there. The light struck his face and showed the slow widening of his eyes.

"Ah-h-h-h, God, what is this? What terrible thing has happened?"

He stumbled forward, was on his knees by the bed when Cleaves reached the threshold. A clutching hand of horror closed over Hal Cleaves' heart. His blood ran cold.

It had happened. That festering, swelling threat of disaster had exploded into reality. Blood on the bed, dripping slowly, awfully to the painted board floor. Blood on the crimson corpse of the woman who lay there. Blood, red and bright, still flowing, still bubbling from slashed arteries.

He forced himself forward, stood beside the kneeling Pierre. The woman—the woman was Pierre's invalid sister, Anne. Dead.

No part of her torso had escaped mutilation. Her formless breasts, withered stomach, her throat, her legs, her face—all criss-crossed with deep wounds. Sodden shreds of a blood-stained bedgown clung to her.

Who had slain her? Why?

"I don't understand," Pierre moaned. Trembling from head to foot, he swayed erect and clung to Cleaves' rigid body. "She was good. Everyone loved her. She had no enemies—"

Cleaves stared, shuddered, said nothing. Enemies? In this grim house, one needed no *motive* for murder! The very walls whispered an insidious command to kill! He knew that now. It was what he had felt downstairs, a few hours ago. This house was evil. It could drive men mad.

"Come," he muttered at last, pulling Pierre to the door. "You must be brave. We must go to the village for help."

It was Paul, the feeble-minded youngster, who felt the tragedy most deeply. How much of it his weakened, fourteen-year old mind understood, no one could know; but the tramping of feet through the house, the questions, the whispered conversations, frightened him. He clung to Virginia, and his large dark eyes missed nothing.

Questions. Answers. A blanket-wrapped body carried from the death-room to another room where the odor of blood did not hang like a foul threat of more horrors to come. Villagers in and out, in and out all morning long, tramping snow from their boots, mumbling words of consolation to Pierre, casting dark looks at Virginia.

Pierre, ill, was put to bed. "Thank God," Virginia whispered to Hal, "we were here when it happened. If he'd been alone with only Paul and the caretaker—"

For two days the village was a bee-hive of whispered opinions. Anne Darnell was buried. Superstitious *habitants* crossed themselves at mention of her name. "Who did it? Who could have done it? She had no enemies!"

At night, the wolves howled in the vast white waste beyond. Doors were bolted; windows were locked. "Whatever it was, it may come again. Dear God, protect us!"

With vague fears in his own heart, Hal Cleaves pitied the people of Dessein in their terror. Never before had horror stalked among them.

"Gin — can't we leave here now? Haven't we done all that's expected of us?"

"No, Hal. Paul, poor boy, needs me."

"He has Lemming, the caretaker. They're together constantly."

"But he needs *me*."

It was not true. Hal knew it was not. With Pierre ill, the boy had turned to Lemming for companionship. They were always together. They read books together in the diningroom, went for long hikes together in the deep snow, played together.

Lemming, forty years old, tall and lean and strong as steel, could easily carry the boy through this trying period of bewilderment and loneliness. Lemming was intelligent, a college man, working here because he loved the cold, the snow, the desolation, and hated big cities. Why, then, was Virginia so determined to stay?

Had this grim place established a hold on her? Was she staying because she *had* to?

PIERRE recovered, went out one night for a walk. It was late, after eleven, and only Cleaves, reading in the livingroom, was up when he left. "I have been sick too long," Pierre said grimly. "The cool air will do me good."

All day long the sky had been a threatening blanket of grey; wind had been whining at the windows. "It may storm," Cleaves said. "If I were you, I would not go far."

"Do not worry."

Alone, Cleaves stared again at the photograph on the old mahogany table. "Five years ago—" Why was the woman's face so disturbingly familiar? Where had he seen it before?

At midnight, Pierre had not returned. Snow was falling.

"He'll get lost," Cleaves muttered. "In bed for so long, he'll feel the cold."

Worried, he went to the front door and opened it, and stepped out on the veranda. The wind stung his face, bit through his clothes and numbed him. The world was all white. Thick, wet flakes of snow swirled in the lanes of yellow light from the windows. The wind's low moan was the only sound in a vast stillness.

"He should be home."

From the rack in the front hall he took a heavy coat, then stooped to buckle on overshoes. The thud of the door as he pulled it shut behind him was muffled by the snow piled at the threshold. The wind reddened his face as he crossed the yard to the barn. It whined after him as he climbed the crude wooden stairs to Lemming's apartment.

He banged on the door. In pajamas, Lemming opened it.

"Pierre is out in the storm. We must find him!"

"Pierre? Out in *this?* Mother of God, wait! I'll get dressed!"

Together, with heads lowered to the wind's increasing sweep, they trudged through the great drifts. Impossible to talk then. Words were torn from the lips, snatched away and shredded. But when Lemming would have turned the wrong way, Cleaves clawed at his arm, bellowed with his blue lips close to the caretaker's ear: "He went north, up the road! I saw him!"

It was bitter cold. On and on, wallowing through the wet waste. Stopping now, to beat with gloved hands at the body, forcing the blood to circulate. Pierre could not live in this! A sick man, he would have no chance!

On and on, stumbling, half frozen. And in the heart of Hal Cleaves, dark intuitions of impending horror took shape, as they had taken shape before. Strong, steel-hard as he was, the intensity of the storm frightened him. It was like a living thing, snarling, determined to drag him down. It was more vicious than the wolves of which the *habitants* of the village stood in constant dread.

Then—Pierre.

The snow had almost covered him; only a leg, an arm, were visible. Face down he lay at the side of the road—if it could be called a road. Lemming saw him first, and was beside him in a stride, stooping to lift the snow-covered shoulders so that the face might breathe.

"Mother of God!" With a strangling cry of horror, the caretaker jerked his hands away and staggered back. And Cleaves stared, for the body had fallen on its side now; its face and chest were visible.

The snow was red. The face of Pierre Darnell was a crimson mask of agony, torn almost beyond recognition. Blood had poured from his gaping throat, from the mangled horror of his chest. Something—something with *claws*—

Pierre had seen it, too, before dying. The claws had not opened his eyes that wide. *Terror* had. Terror had twisted the tongue in his torn, gaping mouth.

Over and over, Lemming was whispering: "Mother of God!" Fear had seized him by the throat. The fury of the storm was forgotten. The caretaker peered with wide, glassy eyes into the swirling murk, as if numbed by the thought that the killer of Pierre might still be lurking, still be hungry.

"We must take him back," Hal Cleaves mumbled. No answer. The caretaker had come no closer after that first backward lunge of horror.

"We must take him back!"

"Yes, yes—" Lemming's blue lips formed the words; the wind ripped them away. But he came no closer.

Cleaves cursed the man, bent alone to the task of getting the body up. Straining, sobbing, he braced his legs in the drift and tugged with both hands. And was suddenly rigid, bending there, staring, for in moving Pierre's legs he had bared a print.

A PRINT in the snow, where the position of the corpse had shielded it from the swirling carpet which had covered all else. But it was no footprint, no mark of a human being. It had deep-dug indentations. It was the print of—merciful God, was he dreaming?—of a monstrous animal!

"Look! Look here, Lemming!"

Lemming shuffled closer. White, now, in the winding-sheet of snow which clung to him, he forced himself to stare. White as something from a grave, or something made ready *for* a grave, he shuddered and uttered a low moan of terror, and shut his eyes.

"A wolf?" Cleaves shouted. "Was it a wolf?"

"In God's name, let's get out of here!" the caretaker moaned. "Take his legs. Let's get back to the house!"

"Was it a wolf?"

"A wolf! Yes, yes! But look at the *size* of it! No ordinary wolf ever had feet so huge!"

Cleaves did not argue. He himself knew nothing of the sleek, hungry beasts who prowled through this desolate region. He was a stranger here. Lemming had lived here and should know. Know—what?

Werewolves? Since the death of Pierre's sister, the villagers had whispered that word more often, crossing themselves as they peered into the north. *They* believed in the existence of werewolves. Were they frightened children, or did they *know?*

"Hurry!" Lemming pleaded. "Hurry!" Frowning, Hal gripped the dead man's legs.

The snow was deeper. The wind whipped them. The way back was endless. When at last the lights of the house glowed through the night, the two men were stumbling white scarecrows, too utterly weary to care. But they clung to their burden, forced themselves on, staggered the last few hundred feet and then up the veranda steps.

In the front hall they lowered Pierre to the floor, stared at each other. A job well done. The door was shut, and the storm's insane voice was a mad roar of frustration. In Lemming's eyes fear burned like a flame.

"I'll get Virginia up," Cleaves mumbled. "We need hot coffee."

Gripping the bannister for support,

he went weaving up the stairs.

How peaceful, how quiet the house was, after the raging inferno outside! How warm! But inside he was cold. In his brain the voice of the storm still shrieked, and a vision of a huge wolf tormented him, its slavering jaws red with human blood.

Wearily he leaned against the door, knocked with half-frozen knuckles. Knocked again.

"Virginia! Wake up!"

No answer. If anything had happened!

The thought was there, and fear fed it. Frantically he seized the knob, pushed the door open. His numbed hand slid along the wall, groping for a light-switch.

There! The darkness was gone. The bulb in the ceiling glowed yellow, throwing its pale wash of light over bureau and chairs and bed. And, thank God, Virginia was in bed.

In it? No—*on* it. Something was wrong here! Dear God, let there be no more horror! She had risen to close the windows against the storm, that was all; and then, half asleep, she had not bothered to pull the sheets over her.

But there was blood!

The fear within him became a raging Niagara as he swayed beside the bed, staring down. His lips whispered her name—"Gin!"—and she did not stir in response. She lay limp, her hair over the pillow, the light yellowing her lovely shoulders. *Blood on her mouth!*

"Gin!" His cry was a wail of anguish.

Dear God, it was not true! The blood was not really there; her lips were not really red with it. Her hands—her hands were not—

His own hand came away wet, sticky. Horror gripped his heart. Sobbing blindly, he seized the girl's shoulders and shook her, and screamed her name. But she slept on.

DEAD? He thrust a trembling hand over her heart, and there was a slow, normal beat beneath the soft breast. No, not dead. Why, then, would she not wake and speak to him? Why would she not explain the blood?

"Werewolf." His own lips whispered the word, and he shrank back, stood rigid, staring at her with horror in his wide eyes. What other answer was there? She had *wanted* to stay in this damned house. She had refused to go away with him. Now there was blood on her cheeks, blood on her hands and mouth. Blood on the floor. Not her own blood!

He had not seen the red smears on the uncarpeted floor before, but was standing now in the crimson trail that led to the window. Like an automaton he paced forward. There were marks on the window where she had opened it. No—where she had closed it, after returning from—

A ghastly moan welled from Hal Cleaves' throat. Again he stared at the girl on the bed. "Oh, my God, *you!*" he groaned. Then, sobbing, he turned and stumbled to the door.

Lemming, the caretaker, stood there on the threshold. Lemming caught him as he collapsed.

There was no jail in the little village of Dessein. Virginia Kelsey was taken to a small suite of rooms above an old stable on the main street. Grim, bearded men with fear in their souls guarded her prison.

"Werewolf!" The word went from tongue to tongue, gathering momentum with the speed of a forest fire. "Werewolf! It was she who killed Anne! She who murdered Pierre! If she gets loose, there'll be more of us murdered! *Werewolf!*"

Crowds of the curious came to look at the mangled corpse of Pierre, and to wander about Darnell's house, staring and muttering and crossing themselves. And gazing with silent suspicion at Hal Cleaves.

"He's her man. Maybe he's one of her own kind—"

Lemming took care of young Paul, taking the boy to his apartment over the garage, where the mutterings and whisperings would not frighten him. Hal Cleaves walked about in a daze, numbed by the hideous thing that had happened.

They found more of the wolf-prints under the window of Virginia's room, where the overhanging roof had sheltered them from the storm. Large, definite prints, ending there at the wall. Cleaves was one of the group that studied them.

"She's a creature of the night! A monster." "She can come and go as she pleases; no prison will hold her!" "Mother of God, we should paint crosses on the windows of those rooms above the stable, to hold her in!"

They did that. They painted crosses on the windows. Outside—for none had the courage to enter her prison.

They fed her by opening the door a scant few inches and thrusting food over the threshold. No one was allowed to talk to her. "Not until we get word from Quebec, telling us what to do!"

In desperation, Hal Cleaves went to Lemming for help.

"My God, Lemming, they're all mad!" He, too, had come perilously close to madness, but that was over now; he was sane again. Only the terror remained. What if these superstitious people let their fears get the best of them? If that happened, they might become murderers!

"They're insane, Lemming. The girl is no werewolf—no more than you or I. That blood on her hands and mouth, I can't believe it was Pierre's. I *won't* believe it! We've got to talk to them, make them understand!"

"There were footprints," Lemming mumbled, "under her window. Wolf-prints, same as we saw when we found the body."

There in the apartment over the garage, Cleaves argued, pleaded. Who else would side with him against the mob, if Lemming refused? But the fear which had burned in the caretaker's eyes at sight of the wolf-prints was still there, still burning.

"If we side with her, they'll think we're in her power. Already they're thinking it of you."

It was hopeless, but in his desperation Cleaves went back, an hour later, with new arguments. The apartment was empty. Lemming and young Paul had gone out together.

He sat, waited. They would be back soon. Gone to the village, probably, for provisions. Waiting, he grew restless and paced the floor. If only he could get some word of reassurance to

Virginia! What must she think of him? They had taken her—carried her—from the house that night, and even then she had not wakened from her unnatural sleep. He himself had not known. Lemming had told him later. He had not seen her since.

Impatiently he stepped to a window, stared along the road to the village. The road was darker now. The sun had set long ago, and night was coming on. Across the way, the home of the Darnells loomed huge and bleak, a grim mausoleum tenaciously concealing its secrets.

What in God's name was keeping Lemming?

He could wait no longer. Something had to be *done*. The villagers, damn their superstitious souls, had kept him from Virginia long enough!

He strode blindly to the door, knocked over a small table as he went. He cursed himself for his own clumsiness and stooped to pick up books, a pipe, a pair of bookends. Hand-carved bookends—some of Lemming's own work. Only this morning, the caretaker had carved out a wooden horse for young Paul.

WHAT a relief it was to think of something other than the horror! But he mustn't be sidetracked that way. In that gloomy prison above the stable, Virginia was alone, needing him.

With dark rage fuming in his heart, he strode to the village.

It was late when he returned, and the rage within him had become a strangling mass of despair. Head down, shoulders slumped in defeat, he climbed the veranda steps and let himself into the house. He closed the door behind him and then sat in the dark living room. Now and then low sobs burst from his quivering lips. There was no other sound. The house was a tomb.

They had refused to let him enter the prison. His arguments had fallen on deaf ears, and his violent outbursts of anger had served only one purpose—to fill their hearts with suspicion. One against an entire village, and that one a stranger; what chance had he?

They were mad, all of them! Terror had warped their minds! And now it was night, and the wolves were howling beyond the village—and that terror would increase through the dreaded hours of darkness. Then what?

How long he sat there he did not know. The silence of the old house soothed his fevered mind after a while, but still he sat. At long last there were voices, and the tramping of feet on the veranda outside.

Frowning at the intrusion, he pushed himself out of the chair and went to a window.

Dear God, what now? Had they made up their minds to drive him out of Dessein? Lanterns were flickering out there in the darkness. Angry faces swam in the pools of light, as bearded men from the village stormed up the steps. Armed men, muttering among themselves, grimly determined about something.

What had he done now?

Beads of cold sweat gleamed on Hal Cleaves' anxious face as he hurried into the hall and snapped on a light. The door was open then; the lanterns and the faces were moving toward him. He stood rigid, clutching the wall, and the sea of surging bodies relentlessly advanced.

"What do you want?"

"You know what we want! It wasn't the girl this time; it was *you!* You and she are the same breed!"

They seized him. He was suddenly the center of a milling mob. Cruel hands jerked his arms behind him and roped his wrists. White-faced women spat at him, cursed him.

"My God, what have I done?"

"You butchered little Rose Ranier, that's what you done. And you know it! Right in her own home! Werewolf!"

Werewolf! Terror iced the blood in Cleaves' veins, calcimined his face. Were they mad? He had not set foot outside the house since returning from the village, hours ago.

"I've done nothing! I swear to you I'm innocent!"

But they were hauling and dragging him out of the house then, and those outside burst into a roar of triumph at sight of him. Savage hands tore at him, shredding his clothes. Blood was hot on his face, trickling to his mouth.

Useless to fight back. Useless to argue with them. Fear of the unknown had twisted their minds, and they were beyond all thought or reason. Someone, or something, had murdered a little girl, just as someone or something had murdered Anne and Pierre. And they were blaming *him!*

It was a weirdly terrifying procession. Lantern-light fell on faces black with rage, on lips muttering and mumbling dire threats. The snow crunched under plodding feet. In the village more faces, more voices, were waiting.

"We'll put him in with the other one. There'll be policemen here from Quebec in the morning, sure. Then we'll be rid of them, thank God!"

"They should be burned. Burned at the stake! Werewolves!"

"No, no, it's not for us to punish them. The law will do it."

"They should be burned!"

The sliding doors of the barn were rolled open. Hal Cleaves was dragged inside, his frantic protests unheard in the surge of the mob's mutterings. Stumbling, staggering from the mauling he had received, he was hauled up steep steps, and a door was unlocked, thrust open at the top.

"Dear God, *listen* to me! I'm innocent, I tell you, just as she is!"

BUT he was thrust forward, fell to his knees. The door closed behind him, and was locked. And he swayed there, tasting the blood on his lips, sobbing out the agony that coursed sluggishly through his battered body.

"Hal!" That was her voice—Virginia's. She was beside him. "Hal, what's happened? What is it?"

She unbound his hands, wiped the blood from his wounds. In a daze he told her what had happened. Then, together, clinging to each other like frightened children, they stood at a window marked with a crude black cross and gazed in terror at the scene below, in the village street.

"They mean to kill us—burn us," Cleaves muttered. "Only a few are reluctant, and they'll be overruled by the rest. It's the end."

"Hal, I'm afraid! Hold me!"

He held her close, his bruised lips on hers. In the street below, lanterns moved like fireflies through the dark. Men shouted. Slowly but surely the mob was increasing. Fear, stark fear of things not understood, had made murder-mad monsters of God-fearing men and women.

"We've got to get out of here!" Cleaves gasped. "Look!"

Dark shapes down there were rolling a barrel across the street. Were breaking the barrel open now, spilling its liquid contents over brush and refuse piled against the stable wall. The roar of the crowd was an unending thunder in which protesting voices—if there were any—were smothered as the bleatings of sheep would be smothered in a hurricane.

"Dear God, they're going to burn us alive!"

Torches flared, revealing the grim, gaunt faces of the men who held them. The mound of kerosene-soaked brush sucked at the flames, then hurled a column of lurid light to the window where the captives crouched. The village street was suddenly bright as day. The mob retreated and was silent with awe.

In that unearthly silence the crackling of the flames drove Hal Cleaves to frenzied action.

"We've got to get out!"

No terror now. He was beyond that. His bruised body had stopped trembling. Wide-eyed, he stared at the door, then hurled himself forward, hurled himself again and again until the ancient barrier splintered from its hinges and went crashing down the stairs outside.

"Hurry, Gin! They won't stop us! The heat out there has driven them back!"

The flames had eaten through the wall. Down there in the stable, rivers of crimson fire flowed along the rotten floor and thick clouds of dirty white smoke roared upward to the ceiling.

"Oh, God, we can't make it, Hal!"

He scooped her into his arms, staggered with her down the stairs into a choking, strangling, blistering inferno of fire and smoke. There was an exit somewhere—somewhere in the awful maze ahead. He had to find it!

Flames licked at the girl's dress, and he beat them out as he stumbled forward. Flames ravenously devoured his own trouser-legs, searing the flesh beneath. Smoke strangled him, blinded him. But he kept going, found the rear wall and groped along it. Then he found a door.

It was not the door through which they had dragged him a short while ago. That one was blocked by an inferno. This was a narrow, flimsy thing at the rear of the stable. Still carrying his moaning burden, he backed into it, using his tortured legs for levers.

The door shuddered open. "Gin! We're free!"

And here there was no mob. Here there were no eyes to see them as they stumbled through deep drifts of snow, away from the burning building. The people of Dessein were out front, in the street.

"My car is at the house, Gin! It's our only hope!"

For an instant they clung to each other, staring back at the raging inferno from which they had escaped. Then they ran, hand in hand, two terrified children fleeing from a nightmare horror. When they cut back to the road, the red glare of the blazing stable was behind them.

The car was there by the house, and the house itself was dark and silent. Cold and exhausted, Cleaves staggered the last few yards and jerked the car door open. In the distance, the sky was a red haze, and the haze was dying.

"Hurry," Cleaves muttered. "If Lemming is here—if he finds us—"

"Lemming?"

"It's he who murdered Anne and Pierre. I have proof. When we're safe out of here, we'll go to the authorities."

She stared at him, doubting his sanity, but he was stumbling around to the other side of the car, to clamber in behind the wheel.

Suddenly he was rigid. From the dark, gloomy building beside them, a shrill scream of terror knifed out into the night! Again and again, like the cry of a tortured animal, the cry wailed forth.

"He's in there!" Virginia gasped.

"He's murdering poor little Paul!"

She was gone before Cleaves could stop her. Without thought for her own safety, she flung herself from the car and sped toward the front door. With a deep breath swelling his lungs, Cleaves blundered after her. The screams in the house had gurgled to a ghastly silence.

He had to go around the car, had to wallow through deep drifts, and in his blind haste he tripped, fell headlong. Precious seconds were wasted while he staggered to his feet again and clawed his way up the veranda steps.

THE front door hung wide. Clumps of snow gleamed along the dark hall where Virginia had rushed in ahead of him. And suddenly her voice screamed back to him from somewhere in that musty maze of rooms.

"Hal! Help!"

And from other lips came a peal of shrill, mocking laughter that jelled the blood in Hal Cleaves' heart as he lurched forward.

Long afterward he was to remember the ghastly scene that met his gaze when he flung himself into the room where the girl he loved was screaming. Long afterward he was to shudder with horror at the thought of it.

The room was dark, but the shape was silhouetted against a window at the far end of it, and Virginia's voice, sobbing now, came from the black depths of a corner just beyond. The shape against the lesser gloom of the window was not Lemming. It was not big enough to be Lemming.

That evil, menacing thing was young Paul!

Giant h a n d s constricted around Cleaves' laboring heart. His eyes bulged, thrusting aside the darkness. He hurled himself forward—but the son of Pierre Darnell did not turn to face him.

The lad had eyes for one thing only: the cringing, helpless girl who stood in the corner. Every fiber of his crouching body was thrilling to her terror. His tongue made wet noises in his grinning mouth, and his eyes were green-glowing pools of sadistic flame in the gloom. His hands snaked up—and they were not hands; they were black leather things tipped with gleaming steel claws! They were hideous instruments of murder!

And then Cleaves was upon him. Cleaves' fingers closed in a wolf-trap grip around the boy's thin wrists.

Writhing helplessly in the clutch of those hands, the boy shrieked out his rage and disappointment, jerked his head around and struggled blindly to reach his assailant with his teeth. Insane with fury, he lashed out with his feet, stabbed at Cleaves' groin with his knees. But he was trapped. Strong as he was, his strength was no match for that of a grown man.

Cleaves hung onto him, flung him

There were footsteps, loud voices, in the hall. But Paul Darnell still shrieked out his mad cacophony of frustration, and was screaming at the top of his lungs when the villagers stormed into the room. To that, Cleaves and the girl owed their lives; for the villagers had come with murder in their hearts and guns in their hands, and would have made more horror if the boy's voice had not penetrated the murk in their twisted brains.

They stared, crowded closer. "Take him," Cleaves gasped. "For God's sake take him! Get these claws off him!"

Then another voice — the voice of Lemming—was audible, and the men of Dessein crowded to the divan to hear a

against the wall and pinned him there. "Light the light, Gin!"

Sobbing low in her throat, the girl stumbled out of her corner and ran to a light-switch. And then Cleaves saw something else.

On the other side of the room, half on a divan and half off it, lay the sprawled, twitching body of Lemming, the caretaker. He, too, had been added to the list of victims. And when the light revealed him—when the glow flickered back from the crimson pool on the carpet—Paul Darnell went suddenly mad with rage.

"Let me go! Let me go! I haven't killed enough of them! Not nearly enough! The little boy in the story killed them all!"

"Listen, Hal!" Virginia cried.

dying man's mumbled words:

"He—did for me," Lemming moaned. "He's mad! His weak brain cracked! He turned against me! When I started training him, months ago, I only wanted revenge on Anne and Pierre, for what they did to my sister. I read stories to him, talked to him. I exercised with him, made him strong and cunning. I made the claws for him and showed him how to use them. It wasn't hard—his mind was already so feeble that I didn't find much trouble in influencing him and—"

The voice sobbed to silence, then was suddenly loud again in a violent outburst of passion. "Anne and Pierre murdered my sister! Don't deny it! She didn't go away from here of her (Concluded in second col., next page) own accord; she was *sent* away, in a raging storm. They said she was unfaithful, but it was a lie, a dirty lie, invented by Anne because she was jealous of Pierre's love for his wife! I'm telling the truth, damn you!

"Later, Pierre repented and went out to find the woman he had sent away to her death in the wilderness. He took another man with him and they found her—and buried her. And from that other man I learned the truth. Now, by God, I've had revenge!"

This time the voice ended in a sputtering, hacking cough.

"He's done for," one of the villagers said.

They stared at Cleaves and Virginia, who clung to each other and bravely faced them.

"We were goin' to kill you. We found your tracks behind the stable and followed you here. I—I reckon we were wrong—"

NEXT morning, as the car fought its way through deep drifts, carrying Hal Cleaves and the girl he loved back to civilization, the girl said hesitantly: "You said you knew Lemming was guilty. How?"

Cleaves had been silent since their departure from Dessein. He had not wanted to talk about what had happened there. Even the knowledge that the son of Pierre Darnell could, with care and treatment, be nursed back to normal again, had not driven from his mind the horrors of the past week.

"It was the photograph," he said. "From the very beginning I wondered —and then I examined the wolf-prints and realized they were all alike, all made with a carved block of wood. I found several slivers of wood in the prints. Lemming was handy at woodcarving. And the face in the photograph —the face of Pierre's lost wife—was *his* face in so many ways. I put two and two together, but even then I didn't dream— Let's not talk about it, Gin."

She pressed herself close to him. The sun was bright above, and the road ahead was a dazzling aisle of white, leading to a new world where tortured minds would learn to forget.

BLOOD
in the
HOUSE

A Complete Novelette of Stalking Doom

By

HUGH B. CAVE

Author of "Twisted Men," "Marked for Murder," etc.

CHAPTER I
The Dead Walk

There was red blood on the

THERE was something unreal about the man. He walked stiffly, and his shoes were like heavy blocks of wood thumping the corridor's uncarpeted floor. In the dark his face was pale, indistinct, the eyes unblinking, the lips unmoving.

Galen Dole, investigator of things psychic, stood quite still, watching him, bewildered by the old-fashioned clothing, the stiff, colorless face that so resembled a death mask.

The man had come from the library at the end of the musty hall. Walking like a tall black shadow fashioned of springs and gears, he slowed to a halt and then spoke. His low voice had the slurred tone of a feebly wound phonograph.

"You are a stranger in this house, sir," he said evilly. "Take warning and go, without further straining our hospitality. We want no strangers here!"

"Who are you?" Dole muttered.

"I *was* Peter Grendell."

The macabre shape moved on again and was lost in deeper darkness. Dole, breathing hard, stood with fists clenched, his eyes wide, until the thumping of the creature's footsteps had died to silence in the depths of the house. Then, pacing slowly into the library, Dole snapped a light-switch and peered around him.

It was a very old library. Aged rugs were scattered on a fine hardwood

---

In that Mansion of Fear, Portraits Drooled

pictures, on the base of the frames, and on the floor beneath

floor leading to shelves that supported more books than a man could read in a lifetime. Large paintings adorned the walls.

As if drawn by a magnet, Dole advanced toward one of the portraits. Then he stopped. Voices were audible in the corridor. Into the room came a tall, slender young man, about twenty-four, and a lovely young woman perhaps two years his junior.

The young man said quietly: "I've told Mary the truth, Mr. Dole. She knows now that you're something more than a friend of mine, and why you're here. She wants to help."

"Yes," the girl said hesitantly, "I want to—help."

Young Will Prentiss gave her arm a reassuring squeeze, turned and left the room. The girl gazed at Galen Dole. Then, shuddering, she turned and pointed to two portraits above an ornate mahogany desk.

"Those," she said, "are the two pictures that—bleed. The old gentleman is my grandfather, the other, my father."

The portrait of her father was the one Galen Dole had been gazing at so queerly. He paced forward, studied the name on the small brass plate

---

a Crimson Warning of Impending Tragedy!

affixed to the picture's frame. The name was Peter Grendell.

Peter Grendell! That stiff, strange figure in the hall! That shadowy shape with the colorless face of a corpse! And the face in the portrait possessed the same sharp features, the same thin lips which had said without emotion: "We want no strangers in this cursed house!"

Moments passed before Dole regained his composure. Then, stepping back, he surveyed the two portraits intently. They interested him. He had heard a great deal about them from young Will Prentiss, who two days ago had come to Galen Dole's New York home and babbled an unbelievable tale of things dark and macabre.

THE ancestors of Mary Grendell, Dole noted, were of the same pleasing mold as the girl herself —except that she, perhaps because of the terror which had been feeding on her peace of mind for the past few days, was less like a flesh and blood young woman than like some pale, lovely ghost wandering through the shadows of this decaying Southern mansion.

But there was blood on the two portraits he stared at. There was blood on the heavy, ornate frames and on the wall beneath, and on the uncarpeted lane of floor beneath that. The blood seemed to have dripped from the portraits themselves!

He walked around the room. There were no windows. There was no door other than the one by which he had entered. It was all very confusing, this business of two very old pictures with blood upon them and blood upon the floor beneath them, and a young man, a very likeable young man named Will Prentiss, frantic because Miss Mary Grendell had suddenly refused to marry him after having promised to be his bride.

"Each night," Dole said, frowning, "these same two portraits have bled?"

"It is more than that," the girl said fearfully.

Dole went to the door and closed it. It might be well if the girl did talk; it might help to relieve her fears. But it might not be well if other members of the household were to overhear her.

Her mother, for instance, had revealed a strange tendency to go prowling aimlessly through the many musty rooms of this old house, mumbling and whispering to herself about things supernatural. And Mr. Andrew Trelaine, Mary's uncle, had been rather obnoxious in his efforts to maintain the traditions of old Southern hospitality.

"Now, Miss Mary—" Dole murmured.

The girl stood with her back to the ornate mahogany desk and stared at him.

"I did promise to marry Will Prentiss," she said. "I loved him. I still do love him. Months ago I told him that my family has been cursed with a terrible, hereditary form of hemophilia for generations, and he said it made no difference. And so I promised to be his wife. Then, we were warned—"

Dole glanced at the bloodstained portraits. "By *those,* you mean?"

"Yes! What else can it be but a horrible warning! This room is locked every night. There are no windows; there is no possible way for anyone to enter except by unlocking the door. My mother keeps the key."

"And have you watched your mother?"

"She and I share the same room upstairs. I know she has not left that room at night. And for the past two nights Peterson has stood guard outside the door of this room."

"Why not inside?"

"Mother will not permit it."

Dole nodded, thinking of the macabre shape he had encountered in the corridor.

"Thank you, Miss Mary." When he had followed the girl from the room, he lingered by the door while she went hurrying down the long hall to the front of the house. Then he turned, re-entered the library.

"Damnably strange," he muttered. "One of the queerest cases I've ever run into."

That was saying something. Galen Dole, New York attorney, adventurer, student of psychic phenomena, had encountered dozens of queer cases during an exciting professional career. Perhaps the gloomy atmosphere of this enormous house exaggerated the weirdness of what was going on here. And yet, that strange shape in the hall—

The house had been a fine old Southern home at one time; that was obvious. Its spacious rooms and corridors had undoubtedly echoed the laughter and footfalls of men and women whose names had since become ineradicable parts of Southern history. The old gentleman there on the wall, for instance—Mary Grendell's grandfather—had been a staff officer of General Robert E. Lee.

And now—the ghosts of a family curse were walking again!

Dole made a slow tour of the library, doing things he had hesitated to do while under the surveillance of Mary Grendell. He moved furniture, pictures. At one end of the room he stood for some time studying the rusted dial of a small wall safe which had been concealed by a heavy portrait of Jefferson Davis.

Later, satisfied that the chamber did have but one entrance, he stood on the threshold and inspected the lock to which, according to Mary Grendell, here was but one key.

"Every night," he muttered, "behind this locked door, those two portraits bleed—"

HE closed the door, turned. Less than ten paces down the corridor, Peterson, the family servant, was industriously winding a man-high clock. The man might have been there a moment or an hour.

"Do you have the exact time, sir?" he asked.

Dole glanced at a watch. "Ten-thirty exactly," he said softly. There was something about Peterson that had inspired his distrust from the very beginning. The man's small, furtive eyes, perhaps, or the apelike swagger of his walk, or his seeming ability to be everywhere at once. Pe-

terson had been the family servant for years.

Dole stopped again when the soft tread of his rubber-soled shoes was disturbed by another sound that came out of darkness at the corridor's end. It was a voice this time, rather high, shrill, but apparently intended to be a whisper. Some people can't whisper; the attempt becomes a parrotlike croak, rather ludicrous.

"Peterson!" the voice called. "*Peterson!*"

Mary Grendell's mother, limping hurriedly out of darkness—

"Good evening, Mrs. Grendell," Dole said softly.

The woman, near-sighted, stopped with a jerk and whipped her head up with a birdlike thrust to peer at him. A strange creature, actually not more than fifty-five, she looked eighty. Her every movement was quick, spasmodic, her voice shrill, her small, twitching body topped by a face which still retained much of its former beauty.

Since the death of her husband, years ago—a death caused by the blood-curse of the Grendells—Deborah Grendell had been slightly childish, queer, believing firmly in such questionable things as communication with the dead, the return of spirits. She spent most of her waking hours in a small room at the top of the house, where with childish zeal she fashioned queer little marionettes.

She smiled sweetly. "Good evening to *you*, Mr. Dole," she chattered. Shuffling forward, she thrust a key into the hand of the servant. "It's time to lock the library door, Peterson. Lock it and give me back my key."

Dole ventured a question. "Just why, Mrs. Grendell, do you insist on keeping the door locked at night?"

"Because that's my Peter's room, Mr. Dole. My Peter always used to sit up late in that room, reading or writing, and he never allowed anyone to disturb him. He wouldn't want anyone to go in there and annoy him now, I'm sure."

Peter. Peter Grendell. That low-voiced, macabre creature in the hall.

CHAPTER II
The Pictures Bleed

THERE was a moon burning yellow above wind-driven scud. Under it, on a stone bench half concealed by magnolia shrubs, Will Prentiss and Mary Grendell sat close together, talking. Galen Dole, wandering about the grounds, saw them but did not disturb them.

He took his time about returning to the house. A light was burning in an upstairs window—the window of the room occupied by Miss Ruth Trelaine. He had met the girl only once, yet was morally certain that she wanted young Will Prentiss for herself.

From that window she could watch the lovers very well indeed. And probably, being a woman, she was even now availing herself of the opportunity to spy on them, even though it increased the pain in her own jealous heart.

Dole re-entered the house and went quietly up the winding staircase. A door opened ahead of him as he went down the second-floor corridor. Andrew Trelaine came backwards out of a room, locked the door and straightened.

"Ah—Mr. Dole!"

"Good evening, sir."

It had taken Dole half a day to get relationships straightened out in this strange house. Now it was simple. This man was Ruth Trelaine's father and the brother of Mary Grendell's eccentric mother. Fat and flabby, he strode forward with his puffy hands clasped behind his back, his chest out like that of a pouter pigeon, his face round and full with self-satisfaction.

He had a right to be satisfied. There was a will, long ago signed by Mary Grendell's mother, which would mean a great deal to Andrew Trelaine when the old lady died, provided lovely Mary Grendell remained unwed.

Dole closed the door of his own room and turned on a light. The light sucked a low, thick voice from shadows near the big bed. The voice ordered Galen Dole to stand still.

He stood where he was, beside a large, bulky bureau which loomed near the door. To his left was an antique desk, open, cluttered with an array of writing implements including a pen, a blotting-pad, a long, sharp, silver letter-opener. The letter-opener lay less than six inches from Dole's left hand, and he was left-handed.

Across the room, in a straight-backed chair beside the huge four-poster, sat Peterson, the family servant. Peterson was apparently left-handed also. His left hand held a large, old-fashioned pistol, and the forefinger of that hand was curled inside the trigger-guard.

"This," said Dole softly, "is a surprise."

There was nothing lovely about Peterson's scowling face. There never had been, for that matter, and at this particular moment the face was twisted much out of shape, revealing irregular front teeth, a lump of thick gray tongue.

"Well?" Dole said.

There was no immediate answer. Peterson was evidently struggling with inner emotions. Stiff as a wooden statue he sat, with his knees splayed apart, his head and shoulders hunched forward, his small feet flat on the floor. Only his hands and the muscles of his twisted face moved; they twitched.

"I never killed a man before," Peterson mumbled. "I don't like to do it, but—"

Galen Dole's left hand shot out and down with the speed of a striking serpent. A man in anything less than the pink of physical condition could not have moved so rapidly, but physical condition was to Dole a major fetish.

So were knives. One room of his elaborate New York home was crowded, in fact, with cases containing knives from all parts of the world. He had long ago learned how to throw them.

His left hand, swift as light, caught the silver letter-opener up by its thin blade, and hurled it. The exertion spun his lean body forward and sideward; the bullet from Peterson's monstrous pistol missed him and gouged a long, ugly splinter out of one corner of the bureau before crashing into the door.

There was no second bullet. The paper-knife, streaking like a light-beam across the room, sank point first into Peterson's gun-wrist. The gun clattered to the floor. Peterson shrieked.

Galen Dole strode forward, seized the man by the throat, lifted him bodily out of the chair and flung him down across the bed. Peterson screamed again.

"Be quiet, damn you!" Dole said, and exerted pressure. The servant's face purpled; breath husked in his throat and he tore feebly at the lean, powerful hands that were throttling him.

WHEN Galen Dole stepped back at last, wiping his moist hands on an edge of the bed quilt, the man on the bed lay moaning and watched with bulging eyes while Dole picked up the pistol and pocketed it. Dole used strips of bed-sheet to bind the man's arms and legs, then dragged him to the floor and with additional strips, well twisted and knotted, lashed him to one of the bed's sturdy legs and gagged him.

The bed was huge, heavy. No amount of squirming and twisting would create enough commotion to summon help. With the room in darkness, Dole closed the door, locked it and stood listening. Apparently the crash of the pistol had aroused no other occupants of the house.

He went silently down the hall. Peterson, before the attempted murder, had been doing guard duty at the locked door of the library. In all probability the man had received his instructions there and was supposed to return there to report success or failure—unless, of course, the murder had been his own idea. Dole descended the stairs and moved across the darkened lower hall.

The corridor leading to the library was black, deserted. He tiptoed down it and stationed himself beside the solemnly ticking clock which Peterson, earlier in the evening, had so industriously set and wound. The library door was a dark, ribbed wall of gloom less than ten paces distant. The house was still as a tomb.

No one came.

Dole paced to the door and put a hand on the knob. The door was locked. The key was probably in the possession of Mary Grendell's mother —at least, it should be.

The big clock ticked on. When it began chiming, the sound was so abrupt and violent in the corridor's silence that Dole stiffened as if struck from behind.

"Midnight," he muttered.

Still no one came.

Two o'clock had come and ticked away again before his vigil was rewarded, and then the reward was tantalizingly vague after so long a wait. Leaning there against the wall, he jerked suddenly to attention, took a short, stiff step forward. A scraping, scratching sound was audible beyond the heavy barrier.

The sound lasted only a moment, might have been made by a cat testing its claws on an uncarpeted section of the library floor. For an interlude of twenty seconds Dole heard nothing.

Then, every nerve alert, he caught the sound of a dull, hollow thud, as if a cork had been drawn from the neck of a wine bottle. The same sound came again.

Nothing else. No sound of footsteps, no further disturbance in the dark. The library door remained closed, locked, and the big house was silent again.

Scowling, Dole removed a long, flat leather envelope from an inside pocket of his coat, extracted a blue-steel jimmy, and, with one knee on the floor, went to work on the ancient lock. A lawyer by profession, his unorthodox methods would have caused raised eyebrows and tut-tuttings of amazement among his erudite companions of the courtrooms, but in half an hour by the big hall clock, the library door creaked open and Galen Dole crept warily into the room.

Replacing the jimmy, he drew from the same leather case a flat, thin searchlight no longer than a man's finger.

A slender beam of white light preceded him, touched the huge ornate desk against the farther wall, rose higher and came to rest on one of the two portraits which, night after night for the past week, had exuded blood.

A muttered exclamation came guardedly from Dole's thinned lips. He turned slowly, aimed the sharp sliver of light into every corner of the room—but the room was empty. Again he stared at the portrait. Red blood gleamed there. Red blood on the picture and on the base of the heavy gilt frame and on the floor beneath!

The blood was wet and sticky to the touch of his questing fingers. He swung sideways, stabbed the light-beam at the second portrait and saw that it, too, was bleeding.

And the room was empty.

Scowling, Dole raised the tiny searchlight and peered into the stern features of Jefferson Davis, glaring at him from the opposite wall. For ten seconds he stood rigid, then very quietly left the room, closed the door and locked it. The locking took time. The big clock was chiming three A.M. when Dole climbed the stairs to his own room.

PETERSON, the family servant, stopped straining at his bonds when the door opened. Eyes wide with fear, he remained motionless, seemed even to hold his breath while Dole relocked the door and strode forward. Dole removed the saliva-drenched gag, pulled a chair closer and sat down.

"Who told you to kill me, Peterson?"

The answer was slow in coming.

"It—it was *him*, sir," the servant mumbled.

"Him?"

"Mr. Peter, sir. Mr. Peter Grendell."

Dole's eyes, watching every movement of the man's quivering face, narrowed ominously and acquired a steely glint.

"He—came out of the library, sir. How he came through the door when it was locked, I don't know, but there he was, right beside me, and when I got over my fright of him he put the gun in my hand and—and told me to kill you."

"Was that all he said?"

"Well no, it wasn't, sir. He said he'd given you fair warning to leave this terrible house."

Dole lit a cigarette. "You believe in ghosts, Peterson?"

"I—I seen *him*, sir!"

"And yet Peter Grendell died many years ago."

"Yes, sir."

"Very well, Peterson. I'm going to let you go, on one condition. I want your word of honor that you'll say nothing of this incident to anyone."

Dole untied him and helped him to his feet. Trembling in every muscle, the little man went hurriedly to the door, but had to wait there, with terror pushing his small round eyes from their sockets, while Dole produced the key. When the fellow had gone, Dole relocked the door, made sure it *was* locked, and went to bed.

The big mansion was silent. Here not even the ticking of a clock disturbed that heavy, threatening stillness. But downstairs there was blood on two portraits in the library, and that strange, macabre reincarnation of Peter Grendell might be prowling again through dark corridors.

"The curse of blood," Dole said softly. "*He* died from it. So did others. A strange heritage, hemophilia, but not strange enough to bring the dead back to life or warn the living of the fate that awaits them. Tomorrow night there'll be an answer. . . ."

CHAPTER III

The Dead Tell Secrets

WHEN he went down to breakfast that morning, Mary Grendell's eccentric mother was sitting alone at the long table in the dining room. The lady looked up, nodded, when Dole entered. Propped in front of her on the table was one of her queer little marionettes, a remarkably lifelike doll that sat with its knees humped, arms folded, alert little head cocked impertinently to one side.

"There was blood," the woman said wearily, as if intoning a ritual, "on the portraits this morning, Mr. Dole. More blood."

Dole professed surprise and concern, but the queer lady had no more to say. Finishing her breakfast in silence, she departed. Peterson, the family servant, served Dole's repast.

Galen Dole thought continually of the two portraits in the library. To these people, he realized, the inexplicable bleeding of those pictures was horribly portentous.

Later in the morning he sensed that brooding terror even more greatly. Outside, the sun was shining, birds sang in the magnolias, yet here in this great house where the blood-curse of the Grendells had driven out laughter, the remnants of a once fine family walked in darkest fear.

The old woman, muttering and chattering to herself, went prowling from room to room, carrying with her the little marionette which had sat so grotesquely on the breakfast table. Her brother, Andrew Trelaine, came and went like a spectre, speaking only when decency demanded it. His dark-haired daughter, Ruth, had eyes only for Will Prentiss.

Will Prentiss and Mary Grendell, always together, were like frightened children walking in a dark forest of despair. And tomorrow, because the girl had insisted on it, Prentiss would go away from here, forever.

Biding his time, Galen Dole learned but one thing of any seeming importance during the long hours of that nerve-racking day. Alone with Will Prentiss in the huge living room, beside a radio which had been silent for days, he drew the young man into conversation.

"You told me when you came to me in New York," Dole said, "that Mary's mother and your father were friends."

"They were more than friends," Prentiss declared wearily. "They were sweethearts. They loved each other, just as Mary and I do."

"And yet Mary's mother married Peter Grendell."

"Yes."

"She and your father had quarreled, perhaps?"

"I don't know. You see"—the young man stared at the carpet, shrugged his slender shoulders—"my father was never one to talk a great deal, Mr. Dole. I suppose they did quarrel. Mary and I have talked about it often. At least, it—it's nice to know that her mother and my father were once fond of each other."

Many hours later, when Galen Dole again found himself seated in the living room—alone, this time, and in the dark—he thought deeply of what Will Prentiss had told him. The big house was silent. Its occupants had retired.

With a cigarette in his lips, Dole went quietly upstairs to his own room. But this time, instead of making ready for bed, he stayed only long enough to procure a small automatic pistol from his suitcase, then closed the door, locked it after him, and tiptoed downstairs again, making no more noise than a prowling shadow might have done.

This time, instead of taking up his vigil near the locked door of the library, he crept across the huge lower hall, through the living room and into a small, dark study beyond. Twice, before reaching his destination, he heard whispering sounds in the darkness behind him, made by the feet of someone who followed. When he stopped, they stopped. Tiny beads of perspiration formed on his face, chilling him, but he kept going.

IN the little study, an outjutting trophy case provided a place of concealment. He wedged himself between case and wall, stared at the door, waited. There were no more footsteps. The person or thing following him had stopped somewhere in the large living room. The house was dark, still.

The tolling of the antique clock in the library corridor heralded the advent of midnight, then of one A.M. Shortly after one, Galen Dole jerked to attention and listened again to footsteps in the dark.

They were not the same footsteps that had trailed him through the house. They were slow, cautious, almost inaudible at first as they descended the carpeted staircase.

Approaching the living room they grew louder, yet were still hesitant, uneven, as if the person making them were afraid of the dark.

They came across the living room toward the door of the study where Dole stood waiting. A white, slender shape was suddenly visible in the doorway, stood there a moment as if afraid to enter. A beam of light spilled through the dark. In the back-glare of the flash, Dole saw the pale, frightened face of Mary Grendell.

The girl was not sure of herself. Dressed now in white satin pajamas that revealed the rapid rise and fall of her bosom, she peered fearfully around the room before entering; then, holding the searchlight rigid in an outthrust hand, and holding something small and dark and blunt in the other, she advanced slowly across the room. Placing the searchlight on a small table, she reached up in the glow of it to pull aside a heavy, gilt-framed oil painting depicting darkies on an old plantation.

Galen Dole watched every move.

With that dark object still clasped in her left hand, Mary Grendell lifted the picture from its place on the wall, then reached up again and removed a small round section of the wall itself. She pulled a chair closer, stood on it. Still she kept peering behind her, as if afraid of being discovered.

Dole saw the girl's slender right arm slide into the wall-opening, heard a scraping, scratching sound, and scowled his understanding. With the fingers of that right hand she was fumbling, he knew, with the mechanism of the small wall-safe whose door was concealed behind the portrait of Jefferson Davis in the library. This room adjoined the library. That was why he himself had come here.

The girl, having removed a section of the wall behind that safe—and having obviously at some previous time removed the rear wall of the safe itself—was now opening that little steel door from the rear!

The scratching sound continued, and Dole knew that the girl was struggling to push aside the heavy portrait which prevented the safe-door from swinging wide. Evidently the door itself, when opened and thrust back, would hold the picture at an angle, leaving a long, tubelike aperture into the library.

Not a muscle of Galen Dole's rigid body moved as he watched the procedure.

Mary Grendell took the small, dark object from her left hand and lifted the searchlight from the table beside her. For a moment only, the thing in her hand was revealed by the glare. It was a small toy pistol, capable of firing corks!

She thrust the searchlight into the aperture—did that, no doubt, so that its light would spill through and illuminate the library. Fumbling a moment with the pistol, she pushed her hand forward, holding it, until hand and wrist were out of sight in the tube.

Dole saw her lean forward to take careful aim, saw her eyes close as the toy pistol went off with a hollow pop. A dull thud, almost inaudible, answered from the room beyond. The girl fumbled again with the gun, took aim, and again pulled the trigger.

When she tiptoed from the room a moment later, the portrait of the plantation darkies was back in its place. Dole, watching her go, did not challenge her. His thin lips were twisted in a scowl.

HE waited until the girl's receding footsteps had died to silence at the top of the central staircase. Straightening from his cramped position he stepped forward, prowled over the threshold and through the big living room. He, too, went furtively through the lower hall to the stairs.

But at the foot of the stairs he halted. Out of the depths of the library corridor came a tall, stiff-striding figure that was hideously familiar!

Galen Dole stood quite still, staring into pale, lifeless features that swelled toward him out of the shadows. It was dark here, as dark as when he had encountered this prowling thing before. In the gloom it was hard to tell whether that face belonged on a living person or on a corpse.

The creature's clumping feet slowed to a stop; the hall was silent again except for Dole's hard breathing. The gun in the spectre's hand was a magnet for his unblinking gaze; so, too, was that shadow-ridden face, the ancient, ill-fitting clothes that hung from a form which might be fleshless and horrible beneath.

"You were warned to leave this house." It was the same low, lifeless voice that had spoken to him before. "You thwarted my good messenger when I sent him to destroy you. Now I shall do what he failed to do, Galen Dole!"

Words came thickly from Dole's lips. "Who—are you?"

"I told you once before, I *was* Peter Grendell!"

"Peter Grendell," Dole muttered. The cords of his throat were tight; his heart sledged furiously in spite of his apparent calm in the face of annihilation. "And you have returned from the dead—"

A man's voice can be a drug sometimes upon the nerves of its hearer. Dole's voice was deliberately pitched low, mumbling words that had no meaning. Then, with the weight of his body shifted suddenly upon one pivoting foot, he hurtled blindly forward!

It was a cunning move, one which few men faced with death would have dared to contemplate. The gun exploded, but did so after Dole's flailing right fist had crashed with bone-splintering force against the spectral arm. Head foremost, he thudded into a flesh and blood target, hurled the man back and tripped him.

For a moment only, the two men rolled on the floor, tore and slashed at each other in frenzied attempts to gain the upper hand. Then Galen Dole's clenched fist made savage contact with the shadowy face of the thing that had called itself Peter Grendell.

A thin shell of clay cracked under his knuckles. The face beneath it, the very human but contorted face of Peterson, the family servant, rolled grotesquely in agony.

Dole swayed back on his knees, staring.

"So, the ghost of Peter Grendell is human, after all!"

He scooped up the shattered clay mask and narrowed his eyes over it. The thing was cleverly molded, hollowed to fit over a man's face. No blundering amateur had made it, that was certain. Only one person in this house of mystery was clever enough to have so closely duplicated the features of the dead Peter Grendell. The marionette woman—

Queer, that the report of the gun had not aroused the occupants of the house. Dole raised his head, peered at the black staircase. The contour of the huge stairwell, perhaps, had muffled the sound. He looked again at the broken clay mask.

"Mrs. Grendell made this," he said softly. "She's very clever at this sort of thing. She made it and told you to wear it, Peterson. Did she also tell you to murder me?"

His hands were at Peterson's throat, kneading flabby flesh. The servant, staring up with terror-filled eyes, moaned a negative reply. The fingers at his throat exerted agonizing pressure. He choked, gasped a more truthful answer. "She—she told me to get rid of you, Mr. Dole! I swear she did!"

DOLE hauled the man erect, saw then how Peterson, though short of stature, had achieved the height necessary for an impersonation of Peter Grendell. The man's shoes were raised with thin metal frames. In the living room, Peterson talked.

It was an interesting talk. Interesting and highly informative. "Mrs. Grendell doesn't want Mary to marry Will Prentiss, sir," Peterson said humbly, rubbing his bruised throat. "Her and Will's father were sweethearts once, and the truth is, she never forgave Will's father for jilting her, as the saying is. She kept it a secret all these years, but I've been with the Grendells a good long time and I know the truth about it. Mrs. Grendell doesn't want any daughter of hers to marry a son of *that* man!"

With amazing patience Dole said softly: "Yet Mary and Will insisted on being married."

"Yes, sir. Even the blood curse— what they call hemophilia—didn't seem strong enough to stop them at first. And it shouldn't, either, because it don't strike very often. Only Peter Grendell has died from it since *I've* been here. He hurt himself and died when the doctors couldn't stop him from bleeding. That's what hemophilia is, sir. A person don't stop bleeding."

Peterson blinked his watery eyes, shrugged dejectedly. "But when Mrs. Grendell saw she couldn't stop Mary and Will, she got desperate. The more she seen of young Will Prentiss around this house, the more morbid-like and—and sort of queer she got about the whole thing. You see, having Will around here kept remindin' her of Will's father."

"And so?" Dole prompted.

"So, when there was no other way to stop it, Mrs. Grendell told Mary she just couldn't marry Will. She said Mary was actually the daughter of Will's own father. *That* meant Mary was Will's half-sister, you understand, and of course—"

"It was a lie?"

"Yes, it was a lie. Will Prentiss isn't no relation to Mary at all. That was just a scheme Mrs. Grendell figured out in her twisted mind. Then—"

Peterson didn't finish. Somewhere in the upper reaches of the house a gun belched; distant echoes lived for an instant in the building's silence, then died. Galen Dole jerked erect.

The thunder of his pounding feet on the staircase was the only sound in the house till he reached the upper landing and went ploughing along the second floor corridor. Then other sounds intruded.

A door jerked open. A man's voice, Andrew Trelaine's, croaked hoarsely: "What is it? What happened?"

Trelaine, in pajamas and trying to struggle into a voluminous black satin dressing gown, came blundering from his room and gaped with white-rimmed eyes as Dole went past him.

Other sounds mingled with the thunder of Dole's feet. Ruth Trelaine's voice, and that of Will Prentiss, flung questions at him. But Dole had reached his objective. The door of Mrs. Grendell's room was open before him. He lurched over the threshold.

CHAPTER IV
The Puppet Woman Dies

IT was a large room, lighted by a pair of bureau lamps held in the chubby fists of wooden marionettes. Mary Grendell had said long ago that she and her mother shared the same bedchamber. The girl's part of the room was evidently the spacious alcove behind heavy draperies on the far side, for she herself was standing there, clutching the draperies, her face white and stiff with horror, her pajama-clad body as rigid as any of the old lady's puppets.

Dole shot a quick glance at her, strode forward and stopped beside the big bed used by Deborah Grendell. The woman lay there, staring off into space.

Her frail body, half covered by bloody bedsheets, was drawn up in a knot, both knees bent to her chin. Her eyes were glassy and her thin face smeared with blood. The blood was spurting from a tunnel drilled in her forehead by a bullet fired at close range.

Dole stepped back, gripping flesh that covered his own heaving ribs. He had come here in a rush; the effort had winded him. Now this other thing was tightening his stomach, making him ill. He raised his head slowly and gazed at Mary Grendell, but the girl said nothing.

He heard Trelaine and the others coming down the hall, swung quickly back to the bed and turned the woman's contorted body to the wall, to hide her bullet-shattered face. Two swift movements of his hands straightened the bedclothes, concealing the bloody stains. At that moment Trelaine rushed into the room, followed by Will Prentiss and Trelaine's dark-eyed daughter, who began talking in a high, shrill voice as soon as she crossed the threshold.

Grimly silent, Dole confronted them. One of them, one of the persons in this room, was a murderer. Every member of the household was here except Peterson, who had been talking in the living room when Deborah Grendell died.

"A very terrible thing has happened," Dole said. He peered again at Mary Grendell. "You must have seen or heard most of it, Miss Grendell. Suppose you tell us—"

"I don't know what happened! I swear I don't!" The girl, still apparently in the throes of very real terror, gazed at her mother's deathbed and seemed about to collapse. "I heard a shot and I—I thought someone was bending over me. Then I heard someone running from the room. I got up and turned on the lights."

"And the room was empty?"

"Yes."

"She's lying!" Trelaine snapped. "Lying!" He swung on Dole, glared as if waiting for Dole to agree with him. "After what you saw to-night, Dole," he snarled, "you should be the first to accuse her of lying!"

"So you," Dole murmured, "were the one who trailed me into the study to-night."

"Yes! And I saw what you saw. I saw this girl's ingenious method of causing those portraits in the library to bleed. She is responsible for what's been going on in this house. Now she denies knowing who murdered her mother!"

Dole moved slowly to the door. "When I entered this room," he said softly, "this door was open. That seems to prove that the murderer ran *from* the room after firing the gun."

"Nonsense! The girl opened the door for an alibi!"

"Then the gun should still be here. Here in the room."

"Yes. And by heaven, I'll find it!"

"Oh, no, you won't!" Young Will Prentiss, face ghastly pale, pushed past Trelaine and stood glaring at Dole. "You're trying to blame Mary for something she didn't do. I'll prove to you the gun isn't in this room. I'll tear the room apart!" He strode toward the terrified girl who stood at the entrance to the alcove. "Dont let them frighten you, Mary. Be brave. I'll show them there's no gun here!"

Dark-eyed Ruth Trelaine said crisply: "Well, show us!"

IT was a strange performance, the others standing very still, refraining from any sort of comment, while a grim-faced young man in scarlet pajamas went noisily from bureau to dressing-table to clothes-closet, pulling out drawers, dumping their contents, snarling while he searched furiously for something he did not want to find.

But when at length he yanked the crumpled pillow from Mary Grendell's bed, he found it.

"No, no—" he mumbled. "Mary, you didn't! You couldn't—"

Black and accusing, the gun lay there. Mary Grendell shrank from it, dropped shakily into a chair and began sobbing. Dole, scowling, took the gun and examined it. One shot had been fired from it.

"So you killed your own mother!" Trelaine said thickly, glaring at the girl. "You—my own niece! *Why?*"

Galen Dole said softly: "Suppose you answer that question yourself, Trelaine."

"Me answer it? What do you mean?"

"Your room isn't far down the hall. You must have found it rather an easy task to sneak in here in the dark, to murder Mrs. Grendell while she lay sleeping. Then, with a few quick steps into the alcove, you were able to thrust the gun under Mary's pillow before Mary was fully awake. Right?"

Trelaine's face paled. "You're mad!"

"You insist that you weren't in this room?"

"I haven't been in this room all day!"

"Curious," Dole murmured, moving slowly sideways to put himself between Trelaine and the door. "Then how do you know Mrs. Grendell is dead?"

Trelaine didn't get it at first. He stood quite still, frowning, then stared mutely around him while his face began sluggishly to lose color. "Why—you *said* she was murdered!" he faltered.

"Wrong again, Trelaine," Dole told him softly. "*You* said she was murdered. You said it before anyone had time to tell you."

"I—I saw the body there."

"Did you?" Dole cast a lazy glance at the shape on the bed. "Seems to me there's nothing there to indicate murder. The woman might be peacefully sleeping. She—"

He stopped talking then, because Andrew Trelaine was hurtling toward him. Trelaine, snarling, came with a bull-like rush, arms flailing, head thrust forward. His route to the door was blocked only by Galen Dole's lean, stoop-shouldered frame which, judging from appearances, could easily be hurled aside!

The man's dark-eyed daughter screamed. Will Prentiss, too far across the room to be of any assistance, nevertheless flung himself forward with a shout of warning. Galen Dole, smiling a little with the scent of combat in his quivering nostrils, dropped abruptly to one knee.

The impact of Trelaine's charging body jarred him; that was all. Trelaine, caught in the embrace of two powerful arms, was raised clear of the floor, and the force of his own wild rush did the rest. Deprived of the floor's support, with added impetus supplied by Dole's sweeping arms, he

shot head foremost, screaming, and crashed against the wall with sickening force.

The man was unconscious and quite bloody when Galen Dole bent over him.

"I think," Dole said to Mary Grendell, "you had better call the police."

LATER, Mary Grendell said humbly: "Yes, it's true, Mr. Dole. When mother told me I was Will's half-sister, I had to find some way out. I couldn't tell Will. I just couldn't! So I tried to show him what a terrible thing the blood-curse of the Grendells was."

Dole nodded. The girl had hoped to send Will Prentiss away without being forced to confess what she believed to be a shameful truth concerning her own birthright. Ingeniously she had resurrected the family curse, had caused those two portraits in the library to "bleed" every night behind a locked door.

The bleeding process had been simple, really. Large capsules filled with blood had burst against the portraits when fired from a toy pistol. The blood itself—which the girl had taken from the bodies of chickens she had killed for her purpose—aided by chemicals ever present in the air, had quickly dissolved the gelatinous containers once they were shattered by the impact.

Mary's own mother must be held responsible for the prowling, spectral shape which in reality had been Peterson. Afraid that Galen Dole might ferret out the truth and frustrate her carefully laid plans, she had tried thus to drive him from the house, at the same time assisting her own daughter in creating an atmosphere of supernatural dread.

Murder? Dole did not believe, even now, that the woman had ordered Peterson to kill him. More than likely she had said, "Get rid of Galen Dole!" and Peterson, misunderstanding her meaning, had, as always, endeavored to carry out her commands.

Dole leaned forward in his chair.

"Your uncle trailed me to-night and saw what you did in the study. He knew that *I* saw you. Knew, too, that with your mother dead, a great deal of money would be yours, to be controlled by him until such time as you might marry. You see?"

"I'm afraid I don't understand."

"It was an easy matter for him to murder your mother and plant evidence that would convict you of the crime. Your actions were already clouded with suspicion. And with your mother dead and you in prison, the entire Grendell fortune would be his."

The girl stared. Galen Dole took one of her pale hands in his and held it a moment, then went quietly out of the room. An hour later, when he left that decaying old Southern mansion and strolled toward the stables to get his car, Mary Grendell and young Will Prentiss were sitting close together on the stone bench in the garden.

Galen Dole, smiling, departed without disturbing them—and took with him, as a memento of one of his strangest cases, the grotesque little marionette which had sat on the breakfast table.

Emperor Blackmail

By Steve Fisher

"Red-eyes" Mark Turner, Honolulu detective captain, thought he was hard-boiled enough to blast a lovely young girl's faith in life—just to convict his man.

MARK TURNER could see that the wild-eyed kid in front of him was a resident of the islands. And he judged by the immaculate quality of her white silk dress that she was probably worth money.

Her greenish eyes were wide. She was damned frightened—anyone could see that. She had bitten her lips until they were creased and red from blood marks.

"I tell you that you must do something!" she pleaded. "It isn't right. Warren has been the confidential secretary to my father, and now he is being held by Su Low. They intend to murder him. I *know* they do!"

Mark Turner, captain of Honolulu detectives, was a huge, well-built figure. He had bright red hair and a crisp red Vandyke beard. The contrast of this coloring, along with the protruding high cheekbones in his face, made his somber eyes as red as glowing coals.

"I can't understand what you are so excited about," Turner drawled. "Your father doesn't seem to want to make any charges."

"But father thinks that Warren was implicated in something concerning Su Low. Warren wasn't. It is all very absurd." Her words were suddenly chopped short. She leaned on the desk, and her long hair caressed her lovely slim shoulders. "How do *you* know who my father is?"

They were on Turner before he could see them.

Mark Turner grinned. He pulled a case of cigarettes from his drawer, put one of the smokes in his mouth and lit up. "Easy," he replied. "You're young enough to be a deb, but you aren't a visitor from the mainland. You've been here in Hawaii for a while. I am assuming that you are important because you are well dressed and rather demanding in what you want. If you were a resident of Honolulu society I should know you. Since I *don't* know you, you must live on the island of Maui with your pineapple-plantation-owning father."

"You're right," she snapped; "but if you think this turning Sherlock on me is doing any good, you've got another guess coming. I'm not sane-minded enough to appreciate such a feat of mental deducing. What I want you to do is—"

"—Rescue your boy friend."

Her small ears became crimson, her green eyes hard. "He is *not* that. He was just an employee of my father, and I am too much of a human being to see any innocent person ruthlessly killed."

Mark Turner stroked his Vandyke. He glanced down at the rather clumsy dragon's-head ring the girl wore on her middle finger.

"I suppose that you're wearing his ring just for good luck?"

She stared hard and long. Her lower lip quivered a little, and then she broke down. "All right!" She glanced about, saw a chair and seated herself in it. "I'm in love with him. So what? I tell you he's straight. A clean, honest boy—"

Turner laughed cruelly. "He's one of the rottenest rats in Honolulu."

She was up again, her small fists tight. "He *isn't* that! Oh, I know the story. You know it too. He was left in China as a baby and brought up under Su Low's care. But he's a white man, remember that, even though his whole life was spent learning the Oriental customs and believing the Oriental beliefs. He was made to be a white Chinese, so to speak. He was educated so that Su Low could use him later in concocting his shady schemes; so he could be used as a wedge to get blackmail letters from rich people. So he could get society women to gamble in the Chinese casinos—"

TURNER put out his cigarette. The girl was serious. The detective knew Warren all right. He was a white "Wu" in the line-up as far as the police were concerned. Although Warren was a square-shouldered young man with vivid black hair and snapping dark eyes, Turner had always considered him as a white rat, because Su Low used him as just that. But the girl was in deadly earnest. She wanted action. Turner wasn't one to spurn a girl's tearful plea; and besides, he had been wanting a legitimate excuse to clamp down on Su Low for a long time.

"I know all about his past," the girl went on hysterically, "but can't you see that it is all due to his raising? He was made to learn everything Chinese. He was hardly conscious of the fact that he was of white heritage. Then he came to work for father, edged into that job. At first he gave Su Low the information he wanted to blackmail father, and then as Warren and I became friends, he ceased doing this."

Turner got up and strapped on his automatic. His reddish eyes were still on the girl, who looked very small in the large chair, talking for all she was worth:

"So I forgave him. I love him, that's why I did it. Don't you think that a man like Warren could change himself completely for love? Don't you think—"

"*If* he were in love," Turner said dryly.

"But he *is* in love! Don't you think that *I* know?"

"I hope you do. Your father's name is Lowell. What do they call you around home?"

"Ellen."

"All right, Ellen. Is the story like this? Warren worked for you, fell in love and refused to give Su Low further information. Su Low captured him and took him back to the lairs they have and is intending either to win him back to his will or kill him?"

Ellen nodded her pretty head vigorously. She got out of her chair, her eyes full of admiration. "Gee," she breathed, "in spite of what I said about that Sherlock stuff, I've got to hand it to you. You know what you're doing, all right."

Turner gripped her hand. "Go on back to your island plantation. I'll see what I can do."

"Go back?" Ellen laughed nervously. Turner couldn't help thinking that she looked like a poppy when her cheeks reddened as they did now. "I'm never going back! Never, see? I'm through with all that. *I'm* changed too. I used to be a little hell-cat around the place. A tomboy who rode horses, acted half savage, and took life as it came. Dad didn't think I'd ever fall in love. And now he—"

"—Is sore because you love Warren, and he thinks Warren is a crook. And he's griped, too, because you are in love at all. So you up and pulled out, and you've probably got a room at the Morris Hotel where he'll find you just as soon as he wants you."

Ellen's greenish eyes were wide with amazement.

Captain Mark Turner rubbed his red beard and grinned knowingly. "You're an all-right kid," he told her. "I admire your grit. You seem to know what you want and make no bones about getting it. I suppose you even want to accompany me down to Su Low's dens—"

"Will you?"

"No. That's out." His voice had a harsh ring of finality. "But don't go back to that Morris Hotel."

He thought a moment. He knew he was a damn fool to let himself become so sentimentally concerned about a crazy girl who had fallen in love with a questionable young man. But hell! A guy couldn't help getting worked up over Ellen's sincerity. Besides that, it was a hot night, and the detective captain's trigger finger felt just a bit itchy.

"No, don't return to the hotel," he repeated. "I don't advise that." He pulled out a card. "Here, take this to the Mama Sans on Beretania and tell her 'Red Eyes' sent you. She'll give you the whole place if you want it. You'll be safe there until I get in touch with you."

There was a mist over Ellen's lovely eyes. "I don't know how to thank you," she said huskily.

Turner bit his lip. "Then don't thank me," he replied. He edged her toward the door, because he could see that she was going to begin crying pretty quickly, and he certainly didn't want that.

CHINATOWN looked eerie. Mark Turner's sure and even steps slapped along the sidewalk ominously. His quiet breathing lent an extra hush to the night. The street was medium-sized. Most of the Korean barber shops were still open, and the slim, slant-eyed females, who were artists at trimming beards—such as his red one—were leaning sleepily against the door-jambs. There were Chinese inscriptions on a lot of windows, but most of the light and noise came from upstairs joints. From those upper windows, gay little banners waved, with crazy black Chinese marks on them; and music that sounded like it was ground from a broken-down hurdy-gurdy shrilled out into the night air.

Su Low controlled a lot of territory, and Turner knew it. He had always wanted to crack down on him, but the rest of the department had disliked the idea. The times when they *had* dragged the astute Oriental in, they had been made laughing matters of in the two daily papers. To venture alone into Su Low's quarters meant perhaps a bullet in the heart, a knife in the side, or a slim silk rope about his thick neck. Any pleasant little thing could be expected, from the death of a thousand tortures to the bleeding of his ears until he'd burst from the pain.

That was why he was crazy. He had allowed his secret brooding to "get" Su Low, and the girl's urgent requests, to swing him into a move that was practically certain to be disastrous. And yet, this way of attacking was the only way he would be liable to stumble upon evidence concrete enough to put the yellow master of Honolulu's evil away for a while.

But "Red Eyes" Turner was that way. As silly as a lunatic at times, but thus far he had managed to keep all of his ribs and both of his arms and both of his legs. So he was lucky. Perhaps he would be lucky again.

He swung down a dark and musty back alley. Pantry boys were emptying stale chop suey into garbage cans. A black cat skirted his path. Thunder clapped in the sky, but summer thunder in Honolulu, and summer rain, meant nothing.

He turned suddenly and went up to the rear entrance of the Morris Hotel. Opening the screen door, he stepped inside. There was a hallway that lead on into the hotel. To his right there was a portal to a "closet." Turner knew that it wasn't a closet at all. It was a room into which one went, to get down into the exotic gambling rooms of the wary Su Low.

Jerking out his automatic, he stepped to the door and tried it. An eye-panel slid back. Immediately a voice rasped:

"Red Eyes!"

As if it had been a signal, Turner crashed forward with his bulky weight. The lock splintered. The detective arrived inside in time to see a trapdoor, which led below, close. He jerked it back open and descended the steps quickly.

He jammed his gun into the back of a Chinaman. Another portal slid open. Turner smashed his way inside. He stared then, all but transfixed at the scene before him.

It was a room of golden radiance. A rich yellow rug was on the floor. Tapestries adorned every wall. Black and red furniture in the lowest, most modernistic design was about, and in the center there were large gambling tables. Casino, roulette, dice blocks.

Well-dressed men and women were standing about. Crooks, all of them. The kind of crooks that Turner couldn't touch. Sneaking into low Chinese dives to have their money taken away from them; disobeying the law so they could get robbed.

For a moment Turner stood swaying on the flat of his feet. His red eyes were burning balls of hatred. The heavy automatic wavered in his right hand. The veins stood out on his forehead.

"Out," he rasped. "All of you get out."

The snooty society-club people bolted for the exits. Turner swept by them and went into the next room. This one was the same as the first. Turner kept on. He came into a small room in which only men were allowed. There were expensive couches on which rich customers slept, doped with damnable poppy fumes.

But Turner had known that he would see all this, and he cared little about it. There was no evidence in it—not enough that could be proved afterward. Hell, hadn't he dragged testimony out of people to prove that *real* opium was used, and that the gambling *was* for keeps, only to have babbling lawyers twist his statements and infer that he had a personal grudge against Su Low? They had said that these dives were but "quaint places with Chinese atmosphere" for the tourists, and that in spite of appearances, nothing was genuine.

Suddenly Turner saw a blade flash across the room. He twisted, and his automatic roared. Simultaneous with the shot came a shrill gong that pierced through each room.

A crowd of Chinamen rushed at Turner and were on him before he could see half of them.

The next thing he knew, the automatic was out of his hand and he was being dragged. He kept telling himself that he was going to get out of everything, and he was going to get this kid Warren out too, if there *was* anything straight about him. Ellen had been so sincere that she had convinced him that there was. And if he could get hold of something valuable in Su Low's office, where he would be taken, he'd clamp the lid on this thing in spite of the big money and "names" that kept it protected.

HE was released in Su Low's office. The walls of this were done entirely in black; the rug was of the same color. Everything was black, in fact, except the grinning little Chinaman sitting behind the ebony desk, his stained yellow teeth gleaming in the light from the lamp.

"Honorable detective come to pay humble Su Low one more visit?"

"Quit the kidding," Turner barked. "I came down to get you to release Warren. I know he turned traitor on you. You had it coming to you."

It was all bluff, but everybody was a *little* afraid of the law, at least.

So Low's grin vanished. His tight yellow face became an evil mask. "Honorable detective puts his nose in too far. You are through, Mark Turner. In China that means—"

"We are in Honolulu, and I am the law!"

"*This* is my China," Su Low squeaked. "Everything your red eyes glance upon here is mine." He chuckled. "You can be killed, your body buried in quick lime, your bones put in a River Street cess flood, and all will be forgotten."

"That's just your version of it, Su Low. But you're crazy as hell, see? You can't kill me. You haven't the guts. You're not as good as you think you are. Warren turned rat on you, didn't he? If that kid wasn't afraid of you, do you think that *I* am?"

"White fool speaks too hastily," Su Low said in anger. He rose to his feet. Turner could see in the shadows behind that he was covered by the guns of Chinese henchmen. "Su Low is all that he says he is. By the power of my most honorable and almighty ancestors, Mr. Red Eyes, you shall die tonight!"

"Warren crossed you," Turner gritted. He was losing his bluff and there'd have to be a helluva fight pretty quickly. He knew that. "If he can beat you, so can I!"

"Crawling reptile! Simpering snake!" Su Low hissed. He jerked open a drawer and waved some papers in front of Turner's face. "A signed statement in full about Warren's love affair with Miss Ellen Lowell. Letters from her contained here, too. A complete blackmail plan. It is all here. Call that a double-cross, honorable moron?"

"Lie, you dog!" Turner shot back, getting his teeth into the thing. He had awakened Su Low's anger which was a rare and hard thing to do. He had to follow it up now, just as a prizefighter follows up with a second good blow after the first. "Lie like the stinking, stupid, withered old man that you are! Those papers—"

Su Low laid them out on the desk. Turner stared down. The Chinaman had been telling the truth all right. Warren had used the girl's love for a blackmail plot! And she had been so sure of his love and his willingness to do the right thing.

Turner lost control of himself in that moment. That was why he was possessed of a greater strength than he had ever known before. He was suddenly a ruthless, bitter and maddened savage, crazed for this devil's blood!

He snatched up the papers and a knife, which lay on the desk as an ornament. Bullets roared out from the partly hidden guns behind Su Low. Turner grabbed the little Chinaman and held him in front of him.

Su Low was fighting like a demon but just one of Turner's mighty arms was enough to hold him.

"Shoot some more, you fools, and you'll shoot Su Low!"

There were no more shots. Su Low struggled desperately, but he was no match for the detective captain. With his red eyes afire, and his flaming Vandyke looking more satanic than ever, Turner demanded:

"Bring in Warren!"

There was hesitation. Turner stayed his ground. He had his back to a solid wall and he was still holding Su Low in front of him. Su Low gave a moaning command in Chinese.

Presently a thin young man came into the room.

Turner wasted no time. His hard eyes surveyed the lad. He saw the grim lines about the mouth; the deceiving eyes that had intrigued an innocent girl.

"Shoot him down!" Turner barked, holding the knife at the back of Su Low's neck. "Shoot him through the head or I'll kill Su Low!"

The slim youth began trembling. Sweat beaded over his high forehead. His eyes got shifty. He made a bolt for the door. Two Chinamen grabbed him.

Turner whispered quickly into Su Low's ear. "Want me to kill you here, dog? If you think I won't do it, you're guessing wrong as hell."

Su Low gave the order to kill Warren without hesitation. The action had completely unnerved the old man's Oriental stoicism.

"Let me live!" Warren screeched in a high voice. "Let me live!" He was slobbering now. His eyes were bulging out. His face was strained and white.

Suddenly he fell to his knees. He was pleading, gibbering, laughing and crying.

"Shoot him," Mark Turner said evenly.

There was a shot. Blood spurted from Warren's forehead. His face ghastly, he pitched forward.

"All right, Su Low," Turner said, "you and I are getting out of this place, and if there's any funny stuff there'll be a heap of Chinese bones in one corner and a lot of blood and brains against the wall!"

"**B**UT you *can't* do it!" the District Attorney roared madly. "Do you realize the names you will have to involve? Do you know how much money there is behind this? I tell you, we've got to release Su Low on bond right now!"

"I've listened to you too damned long," Mark Turner said acidly, extracting a cigarette from his case and tapping it on his mahogany desk. "As Su Low told me, I'm through. Through listening to you and a lot of other people around here, see? I'm keeping Su Low behind bars. Got the governor's okay on it, and if you don't like it, you can—"

"But the case will be absurd in court, just like the last one. You have no proof for your statements. And if this turns out to be a foul ball too, you're *through* all right!"

Turner's red eyes had a peculiar gleam in them. "So my reputation is at stake, is it? Well, so what, you big baboon? I have the evidence I need this time. I don't have to have you to tell me that it has to be good evidence. And I don't want to listen to your jabbering that the papers are riding me and calling me crazy. Su

Low stays in jail until this court trial opens!"

The D.A. shrugged. "I'm sure they'll run you the hell out of town on a rail!" He jammed on his hat and left the office.

Turner sat gazing at his burning cigarette. As the smoke swirled upward he realized that he was a stubborn fool, trying to go against politics for the right of law. But he had the goods now. He had risked his life to get the goods last night, and hell, he'd use every shred of evidence—

The door of the office opened. Turner's heart sank. This was something he had not considered. Ellen Lowell walked in. Her face was white, chalk-white. Her soft hair was still down about her shoulders. She wore black—a lovely mourner, she was.

"They killed him before you could help him, didn't they?" she asked in a strained voice, coming over to the desk.

Turner ducked out his cigarette. He got up and came around the desk. He took Ellen's hand; it was very soft. He tried to speak to her but found he couldn't. His mouth was hot and dry. He stared down at her sweet beauty. Of course, she didn't know about that double-cross. It was Turner's ace in the hole for the trial. He was keeping mum about it.

He didn't want to say what he had done. But he couldn't help it, talking to the girl like this. She was a "right" kid all right, and there wasn't any getting around that.

She looked up at him, her babyish face soft, tender. "But Warren died thinking of me, I hope," she managed. "He was like that. I'll bet he died bravely and proudly. Stood right up and took his medicine."

There was an ugly picture in Turner's mind. It was that of a slobbering idiot down on his knees, gibbering for his life.

"After we discovered our love," Ellen went on in a trembling voice, "he changed so much. He was so straight and staunch and loyal. I shall always adore that in him. How wonderful he was—"

A tear trickled across her cheek.

The hard detective with the red Vandyke turned away. He glanced toward the window. His voice was hollow and dry. "Yeah, you're right, kid. Warren stood up, and when they burned him down he said—"

"Yes?" Her voice was pitifully eager.

It was no use. Turner couldn't let her know. "He told them to tell you that he loved you, Ellen, dear—even in death!"

She breathed deeply. A radiance flushed from her cheeks. She went to the window, and then turned about. Her lips were firm, her green eyes steady.

"This," she said, "is the one thing in my life that means something. I'll go back now and be a tomboy and a savage again. No more love for me." Her eyes softened. "So he said that even in death—" She burst into tears. Choking back sobs, she concluded: "He was so wonderful! So *darned* grand!" She ran from the room.

MARK TURNER sat down a moment. He was too dazed to think coherently. Evidence! Newspapers laughing! Running out of town! Railed out! Fruitless years of detective work in Honolulu all powdered to hell now for a statement a dying coward didn't make!

He got up and went to the window again. His red eyes stared out into the street. Was it worth it all? Was her love and life worth more than his reputation, his job? Of course it wasn't. She was just a kid and she had a lot of life before her. The romance was her own fault; she should have listened to her father. Turner would send the evidence in, the papers that would reveal the truth about Warren to her. Sure, he would, because he wasn't a sucker to women. Not Mark Turner. Some other soft-hearted guy, maybe, but not the famous "Red Eyes" of Honolulu!

He shrugged indifferently and lit a cigarette. He was still at the window watching. What a sap he would be not to turn in the evidence! To keep it in his safe where it now was. Or to burn it up. Hell, he couldn't convict Su Low without it, and he knew he couldn't. And without it now, he couldn't remain in Honolulu as a detective captain and face the music.

Suddenly his eyes hardened. He saw the slim figure of the girl as she left the police station and climbed into the waiting automobile. Her father, a white-haired old man, was holding the door open for her. She looked very sweet and pure there in the sun.

Mark Turner threw down his cigarette and stepped on it. He crossed the room and brought out the papers he had taken from Su Low's place. Quickly, with shaking hands, he struck a match.

The ashes floated to the floor. The man with the red Vandyke and the burning eyes of a living Satan laughed hoarsely. His diabolic laughter echoed from the walls and shrieked back into his ears.

Those ashes on the floor were his ashes. He was through. All done, because his heart, which had escaped so many bullets, wasn't as hard as he thought it was.

His hands numb he picked up the phone and got the outside desk.

"Hello, sarge? Book me on the *Mahona* sailing tonight for the mainland. And tell the D.A. I was just kidding about last night. I was drunk. He can release Su Low and let him go his own stinking way."

Turner was just about to hang up when the voice of the sergeant poured excitedly over the wire to him.

"*What?*" he gasped.

"Yeah, that's right," the sergeant told him. "Su Low knew that you had the goods on him this time, and you know these Orientals—he committed suicide in his cell."

When Mark Turner was at last able to speak, he said weakly, with his voice trembling:

"Cancel those mainland reservations and get a plane to take me to Maui. I guess I'll—I'll get a little rest playing tomboy with a girl named Ellen."

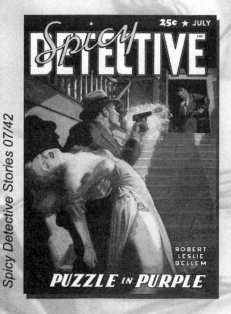

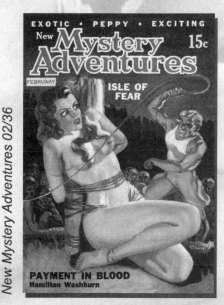

#89
Jim Anthony
July 2006

#90

The Black
Bat #1
Sept. 2006

#91

Phantom
Detective
Nov. 2006